W9-CAB-629

THE 2nd BEST HAUNTED HOTEL

on MERCER ST.

BY
CORY PUTMAN OAKES

ILLUSTRATIONS BY
JANE PICA

AMULET BOOKS
NEW YORK

THE 2nd BEST HAUNTED HOTEL on MERCER ST.

Cataloging-in-Publication Data has been applied for
and may be obtained from the Library of Congress.

ISBN 978-1-4197-4017-6

Published in 2020 by Amulet Books, an imprint of ABRAMS.

Printed and bound in U.S.A.
10 9 8 7 6 5 4 3 2 1

Amulet Books are available at special discounts when purchased
in quantity for premiums and promotions as well as fundraising
or educational use. Special editions can also be created
to specification. For details, contact
specialsales@abramsbooks.com or the address below.

ABRAMS The Art of Books
195 Broadway, New York, NY 10007
abramsbooks.com

IN LOVING MEMORY OF BOB OAKES

CHAPTER 1
WILLOW

The ghost would have been a head taller than the girl—if the ghost had a head at all.

Instead, the ghost had a stump. It was right between her shoulders, marking the spot where her neck used to be. The stump was framed by several lacy shirt collars that were so stiff with dried blood they stuck up at weird angles.

The ghost's long skirts billowed as she silently floated up behind the girl. The sharp spurs on her leather riding boots dangled in midair as the apparition slowly stretched out her arms.

The girl was busy straightening a display of brochures on the mantel while balancing a stack of towels on her hip. She didn't see the ghost.

The ghostly woman rose even higher into the air. Her long coat blew back in an unseen wind. She leaned closer to the girl. The ghost's milky-white fingers were inches from the girl's light brown curls . . .

. . . when the tip of one of her spurs caught on the handle of a basket of firewood.

The ghost careened into an end table, which wobbled dangerously. It didn't fall over, but the brass candelabra and two picture frames on top of it went crashing to the floor.

"Molly," the girl said without turning around. "Haven't we talked about you going headless in the lobby?"

"Sorry, Willow," Molly said. Her boots floated back down to the ground.

Willow Ivan had never been able to work out how Molly, the Hotel Ivan's resident Headless Horsewoman, was able to talk when she was not always in possession of a mouth. Or a tongue. Or vocal cords. Somehow, she managed.

Pity the same couldn't be said for her eyesight.

Molly knelt down and felt around blindly. When she found the candelabra, she set it back on top of the table. Two of its three candles had snapped in half, and Willow made a mental note to replace them later. After she put away the towels, and signed for the linen delivery, and fixed the toilet in room eight.

No, maybe before she fixed the toilet. The lobby needed

to look nice. Willow kicked the broken candle halves under the couch, then picked up the two picture frames—unbroken, luckily—and set them back on the table.

"I'm sorry," Molly said again. "I can go . . ."

"Don't be silly," Willow said, holding her breath as Molly's skirts swayed perilously close to a shelf full of breakable knickknacks. "Just be careful, OK?"

"Sure thing," Molly agreed, feeling her way around the coffee table. "What I really need is—"

"To find your head?" Willow suggested hopefully, looking around. "It can't be far. Last time it was in the pantry, wasn't it? Or maybe the dining room?"

"—someone to mope with," Molly finished. She collapsed onto the overstuffed red sofa and patted the cushion next to her. "What do you say?"

Willow sucked in a breath. "So, you've heard, then?"

"About Anna? Yes, dear. We've all heard."

"From Dad? He said he was going to call a meeting."

"No, dear. I heard it from Pierce. I don't think there was a meeting."

Willow frowned. Last night, after years of Fading, Anna Winthrop, the Hotel Ivan's housekeeper, had finally progressed to the final phase of the ghost death cycle and Moved On. Willow had been up with her all night, trying to make her transition as peaceful as possible. Her dad had promised to speak with the staff about Anna's passing first thing in the morning. He must have forgotten.

And now it seemed there was no point.

Towels. Linens. Candles. Toilet.

"Anna's been Fading for as long as I can remember, but I never thought she'd actually just be . . . gone," Willow said wistfully. "She had her Last Gasp around midnight—she dusted the entire first floor and cleaned every dish in the hotel. After that, she just sort of . . . disappeared. Did you know that when she was alive, she used to work in the castle of King Henry VIII?"

"Yeah," Molly said skeptically, and Willow got the feeling that wherever her head was, her eyes were rolling. "That's what she always *said* . . ."

"You don't believe it?"

"Let's just say she wouldn't be the first ghost to try and make her life sound more interesting than it actually was. Now that she's gone, who will do the housekeeping?"

Willow shrugged and readjusted her stack of towels. "Me, I guess."

"Really?" Molly sounded skeptical again. "Don't you already have enough to do? With school and every—"

"I've got everything under control," Willow assured her. "The hotel is doing great. We're full—all twelve rooms! We're booked up for dinner. Plus, our *Zagged* rating is through the roof! I checked it first thing this morning, and we're up to four and three-quarters stars!"

And Dad was wearing shoes yesterday, Willow added silently to herself. *Real shoes. The ones with the ugly tassels.*

The ones he used to wear when *he* had been the one worrying about the linens, busted toilets, and towels.

Willow opened her mouth to tell Molly this, but she was interrupted by a soft chime from the back of the hotel.

"That'll be the linen delivery. Right on time," Willow said, swinging around to grin triumphantly at Molly. "See what I mean? *Under control!*"

"If you say so," Molly said, still sounding unconvinced. "Willow?"

Pierce, the Hotel Ivan's concierge, appeared in the doorway.

Francisco Pierce was everything a concierge at a haunted hotel should be: polite, efficient, and just snobby enough to lend the place an air of quality. His pasty face was usually fixed in a mild frown, and he was inevitably dressed every bit as sharply as he had been on the day he died—more than three hundred years ago.

"The Fosters are checking out."

"Now?" Willow squeaked, checking her phone. It was six thirty in the morning. "I thought they were leaving tomorrow? Why—?"

"I don't know. But they're demanding to speak to someone *Living*." Pierce rolled his eyes at the outrageousness of such a request as the back door chime rang for a second time.

"Bree!" Willow called, catching sight of the Hotel Ivan's office manager/social media director. "Would you mind—"

"Wi-Fi's down again," Bree muttered as she speed-walked through the lobby toward the cabinet where they kept the router. "I do *not* have time for this if I'm going to get today's Instagram post up!"

Bree, a pretty black woman in her mid-twenties, was one of the youngest ghosts at the Ivan, both because she'd died so young and because her death era (the 1960s) was so recent. Her hair was almost always styled in the same large Afro she'd worn in life, and she was never without her Nikon camera, which hung from her neck on a sparkly purple strap.

"Besides," Bree continued, reaching into the depths of the cabinet, "you know the linen service won't accept a ghost signature."

Not liking her options, Willow walked resolutely to an office door marked HOTEL IVAN STAFF ONLY and flung it open.

"Dad?"

The office was cluttered and cramped, and Willow's father sat hunched over a desk in the corner. His face was bathed in the light of an ancient computer monitor. Willow realized with a start that her father's pale complexion was starting to look every bit as pasty as Pierce's.

"Busy," he said.

"Could you help for a sec? The linens are here, and I also have guests checking out. I need somebody Living . . ." Willow stumbled to a stop. Her father's eyes hadn't left the computer screen. And there were slippers on his feet today. Fuzzy, worn, cotton slippers. The ones with a hole in the left heel.

"Did you go to your appointment with Dr. Strode yesterday?" Willow asked, knowing the answer even before her father shook his head.

"I was busy. I'll go to the next one."

"OK," Willow muttered, and closed the door.

The door chime rang a third time, Pierce started tapping his foot, and Willow stared at the pattern of the wood grain above the door handle, wondering what to do. Finally, she heard her mother's voice inside her head.

Guests always come first.

"Right." Willow dumped the towels into Pierce's arms, ran a distracted hand over her curls, and headed to the front desk.

"Can I help you?" she said to the impatient couple waiting there. "The Fosters, isn't it?"

"Yes. Are you in charge here?" Mr. Foster asked. He was tall and mostly bald. He and his wife were both blinking uncertainly at Willow.

"Yes, I am," Willow answered, and paused, giving them a moment to adjust to the idea of a twelve-year-old in a position of authority. Most adults needed a moment for that, she had found. "What can I do for you?"

"We're checking out," Mr. Foster barked. "Immediately."

"Is there a problem with your room?" Willow asked in her most patient voice. "If it's about the toilet, I've been meaning to—"

"It isn't the toilet," Mr. Foster said snippily. "It's more . . . the general atmosphere."

"The atmosphere?"

"We thought it would be scarier!" Mrs. Foster cut in, looking a tad embarrassed to have said that out loud.

"Scarier?" Willow repeated.

"Yes." Mr. Foster pulled a crumpled Hotel Ivan brochure out of his pocket. "We were under the impression that this was a *real* haunted hotel."

"It is," Willow said. She gestured over her shoulder at Pierce, who was hiding the stack of towels behind the front desk and who was noticeably more see-through than any Living soul possibly could have been.

"A real *scary* haunted hotel," Mr. Foster amended. "It says here that guests can expect to be awakened every morning by one of the top ten Phantasms on the East Coast."

Willow turned to Pierce. "Leo didn't do his show this morning?"

"Oh, he did it," Pierce said, looking uncomfortable. "It . . . well, it might not have been his *best* performance . . ."

"And we prepaid for the sunrise trail ride with the Headless Horsewoman this morning, but she never showed up," Mr. Foster added.

Willow looked accusingly toward said horsewoman, who was currently splayed out on the lobby couch. "Molly!"

"You told me not to take any guests out when I can't find my head!" Molly shouted back. "Not after what happened last—"

"OK, OK," Willow interrupted quickly before the Fosters could hear the rest of that story.

"And here it says we can expect to 'frolic with one of the oldest ghost hounds in Vermont,'" Mr. Foster continued, then glared over the paper at where his two children were kneeling on the floor. They were giggling and taking turns passing their hands through what looked like an enormous, slightly see-through cotton ball with legs. "I thought the hound would at least be menacing. Or flesh-eating. Or *something.*"

"You mean Cuddles?" Willow asked.

Hearing his name, the cotton ball rolled to his feet. Then he scampered over and sat primly in front of Willow, not looking the least bit menacing or hungry for human flesh.

"The hound's name is *Cuddles?*" Mr. Foster growled.

"Yes," Willow said as Cuddles turned his attention to Pierce, who produced a treat from a bag labeled GOOD GHOULS: TREATS FIT FOR THE LIVING (BUT NUTRITIONALLY BALANCED FOR YOUR DECEASED PET). "We call him Cuddles because . . . well . . ."

"Because he likes to cuddle," Pierce finished with as much dignity as possible given that Cuddles had jumped into his arms, devoured the treat, and was now licking his face.

"Cuddling is *not* scary," Mr. Foster insisted. His face started to turn red with frustration. "Nothing here is scary. I mean, look at *her!*" he pointed toward Molly. "She's head-less! She could be scary. Terrifying, even . . . if she was doing anything interesting. But she's not! She's . . . what *is* she doing?"

"She's moping," Willow answered.

"Moping is not scary!" Mr. Foster raged, his face turning even redder.

"Sir," Willow tried, "this is a family-run hotel. It's quite old. Most of our ghosts have been haunting this property for—"

"—centuries," Pierce cut in proudly, tucking Cuddles under one arm.

"Centuries?" Mr. Foster sounded skeptical.

"I started working in the kitchens here in the winter of 1619," Pierce informed them icily. "Died in a kitchen fire in 1656. Was promoted to butler in 1670 and then to concierge in 1694, a position I have held ever—"

"Yes, yes. That's very impressive. But it is not, in fact, *scary*," Mr. Foster maintained.

"What *would* be scary to you, sir?" Pierce asked.

"Well . . ." Mr. Foster began thoughtfully, then cut himself off and elbowed his wife. "There! Look!"

Willow turned to follow his gaze.

A ghostly apparition had appeared on the stairs to the right of the front desk. It was a woman wearing a white nightgown that seemed to float around her as though she were underwater. The nightgown and her pale skin were both so translucent that Willow could see the stairway behind her. Her curly brown hair was in disarray, and her hollow eyes darted from side to side, fixing on everything in turn but nothing in particular, as she drifted slowly down the steps.

As the ghost entered the lobby, a feeling of heaviness came with her. To Willow, it felt like a thick cloud had washed right over her from her eyeballs down to her toes. It seeped in through her nostrils and reached down her throat, choking her.

A sob escaped the woman's throat, and Willow swallowed, feeling a strong urge to cry herself. Instead, she took a step backward and looked anxiously toward the Fosters. But they didn't seem affected by the grief cloud.

"A Weeping Woman!" Mr. Foster marveled, then fumbled to get his phone out of his pocket. "Kids! Go stand by her! Quick, now—"

"No!" Willow shouted.

Cuddles barked in Pierce's arms as the kids scrambled toward the stairs. The apparition appeared not to notice the commotion, but Willow moved quickly to place herself between the woman and the Fosters.

"She's *not* a part of the hotel guest experience," Willow said firmly, holding her arms out wide to ruin any pictures. The kids groaned in disappointment, and Mr. Foster's face screwed up with anger once more.

"I'd be happy to give you a refund, sir," Willow assured

him hurriedly. The floating woman let out another sob and drifted toward the front desk.

"Fine," Mr. Foster said irritably. "But we won't be staying here again. When we come back to town, we'll be staying at a Hauntery. *They* know how to make things scary!"

"*And* their toilets always work," Mrs. Foster added nastily, gathering up the children.

"The Hotel Ivan is the only haunted hotel in Mercer," Willow called after them. "There's no Hauntery within a hundred miles of here."

"Thank goodness," Pierce muttered.

The Fosters slammed the door behind them.

Willow took a step toward the back door, then realized that the doorbell had stopped chiming some time ago. She'd missed the linen delivery. She should probably still go fix that toilet in case somebody checked in later. So much for having everything under control.

Willow turned to the Weeping Woman. She was behind the front desk now, still looking lost but also strangely as though she belonged there. She had stopped sobbing. She blinked, then looked up.

"Willow?" she said.

Then she blinked again, and the spark of recognition in her eyes faded into confusion once more.

Only one thing comes before guests, Willow, and that's family.

"Hi, Mom," Willow said with a sigh. "Let's get you back to your room."

CHAPTER 2
EVIE

The Mercer Street Hauntery looked exactly like every other Hauntery Evie MacNeil had ever seen—and she'd seen *a lot* of them.

Each Hauntery property had the same (intentionally) squeaky iron gate that spanned two (artfully) crumbling brick pillars. The hotel itself—a sprawling, squatting Victorian mansion—had the same faux-marble columns in front as all the others. The usual two-story, latticed, southern-style porch wrapped around two sides of the building. The fake gravestones in the well-manicured grass were purposefully weathered and knocked at angles that conformed perfectly to Corporate guidelines. The soundtrack playing when you entered—a mixture of spooky sounds and organ music—had been certified by a panel of psychologists as fear-inducing and was required to be played on a constant loop in all Hauntery lobbies.

The carpet was the same in each Hauntery, too. And the three-quarter lighting, spooky portraits, and ghost staff's uniforms were all rigidly regulated by Corporate to be exactly the same in every property around the world.

The ghost staff quarters were no surprise, either. Hidden behind all of the finery of the public spaces, they were identical to the dull, dingy, depressing rooms that Evie, her mother, her father, and her cousin Louise had called home at every other Hauntery they'd ever worked at.

Since *everything* was the same, Evie couldn't explain why *she* suddenly felt different.

But she did. The moment she'd walked through the gates of this particular Hauntery, she hadn't been able to shake the strangely anxious feeling that had come over her. It got steadily worse, even after they met a nice, bubbly member of the ghost staff named Patricia Spengler, who showed them to their rooms and complimented Evie's maroon Dr. Martens.

Patricia left far too soon, and when Evie's mother announced that it was time for them to change and rehearse their acts for the hotel manager, Evie knew she Just. Couldn't. Take. It. Anymore.

"No," she said.

Her mother didn't hear her. She had already turned away and was fussing with the fastener on Evie's father's Phantasm cloak.

"You'll be brilliant, darling," Evie's mother cooed to her husband. "The most frightening Phantasm this town has ever seen."

"And you, my dear, will be the most hauntingly beautiful Weeping Woman, as always," he cooed back.

"No," Evie said again, louder this time.

"What did you say, dear?" Evie's mother asked, but before Evie could repeat herself yet again, Louise bounced into the room. Evie's cousin was already dressed and ready to go, clad in a pink pinafore dress with a white lace collar, tasseled knee socks, and shiny Mary Janes. Her curly red pigtails bounced with every skipping step, as did the floppy, oversize, bubble-gum-pink ribbons on either side of her head.

The sight of Louise made Evie want to vomit. But Evie's mother's face lit up with a giant smile.

"Oh, Louise, you look *adorable*. Simply adorable. Jim, doesn't she look *adorable*?"

"Adorable," Evie's father agreed.

"Come, come, Evie." Evie's mother clapped. "Let's have a look at the most *adorable* Spooky Little Girl ghosts on the Eastern Seaboard—Louise, are those ribbons in your hair?"

"Yes, Aunt Karen." Louise swung her head from side to side, making the ribbons smack against her cheeks. "I just added them. What do you think?"

"Adorable," Evie's mother gushed, and Evie was certain she was going to scream if she heard that word again. "Evie, dear, do the ribbons! Do the ribbons like Louise!"

But Evie didn't do the ribbons. Or the dress. Or the socks. Or the shoes. Not because she couldn't—in fact, being able to change her clothes and hairstyle in the blink of an eye was one of the only things Evie actually liked about being a ghost. She did it all the time; today, she had changed her naturally straight red hair to wavy gray with blue streaks. Usually, she changed into her performance outfit every evening without complaint.

But not tonight.

"*No,*" she said again, wondering how many times she was going to have to repeat herself before somebody actually heard her.

"You don't like the ribbons?" Louise asked innocently.

Evie narrowed her eyes at her cousin, who, she was sure, had thought up the ribbons solely to torture her.

"I don't want to wear those," Evie said dangerously.

Evie's mother sighed. "Fine, fine. Forget the ribbons. But do change the rest of your clothes, Evie. The manager will be here any moment to check us over for the test run tonight."

Evie shook her head. "I don't want to wear *any of it*," she clarified. "I don't want to be a Spooky Little Girl anymore. I want to be a Terrifying Phantasm, like Dad."

Evie's mother sighed again.

Evie's father stepped forward. "Evie, we've talked about this—"

"*You've* talked about this," Evie corrected him. "I never get to say any—"

"We all play our roles," Evie's father interrupted. "We scare the guests, and their fear helps us to remain on this plane of existence. It allows us all to stay together. It's a good arrangement, Evie."

"But Dad, I can *be* a Terrifying Phantasm. I've been practicing! I could inspire much more fear doing that than—"

"Why would you want to do that," Evie's mother interrupted, "when you're so wonderful at being a Spooky Little Girl?"

"Just because I'm good at being a Spooky Little Girl doesn't mean I can't do other things, too," Evie pointed out. "I *want* to be a Terrifying Phantasm. I can do it, I know I can—"

"You can't," Evie's father cut in. "I'm sorry, but you can't. It's not you."

"How do you know it's 'not me' if you won't even let me show you what I can—"

"*Enough!*" Evie's father thundered, summoning enough of his Phantasm voice to make the rest of them stand up straighter. "I'm tired of having this argument. You are a Spooky Little Girl. You're lucky to be a Spooky Little Girl. You are a Hauntery ghost. And why are you lucky to be a Hauntery ghost?"

Evie gritted her teeth and refused to say it. With Louise around, she knew she wouldn't have to, anyway.

"Because *Hauntery ghosts never Fade!*" Louise proclaimed loudly.

"*Hauntery ghosts* never *Fade!*" Evie's father repeated, smiling down at Louise before turning back to Evie. "Now, I don't want to hear another word about this Phantasm nonsense. Is that understood?"

Evie opened her mouth to say quite a few more words about it, but Louise stepped up right in front of her face, grinning nastily.

"*I* can get her ready, Uncle Jim," she offered, staring pointedly at the left side of Evie's head.

Evie gasped as she felt one side of her hair spring up into a pigtail.

"Stop that!" Evie shrieked at her cousin, closing her eyes

and not opening them again until her hair was back to its wavy gray with blue streaks.

"Girls!" Evie's mother admonished them. "We don't have time for this."

"They'd *laugh* at her if she tried to be a Phantasm," Louise spat, curling one of her pigtails around her finger. "All the guests would just laugh and laugh."

Evie ground her teeth and pondered, for the billionth time, how cosmically unfair it was that she was stuck with her hateful cousin for all of eternity. Ever since they'd all died together in that car accident, Evie's parents had declared that Louise was "like another daughter to them." Nobody had ever asked Evie how she felt about gaining a sister. She definitely had thoughts on the matter.

"They wouldn't laugh at me," Evie informed Louise.

"They *might*," Evie's mother declared, coming between the two girls. She was starting to look less annoyed and more worried by the moment. "And then what? At the very least, we'd lose our jobs at the Hauntery—and you know how hard we've worked to make it here. There's a line of ghosts a mile long waiting to fill our positions. And at worst, you might start to Fade! Maybe even enough that you'd Move On! Without us!"

Evie's mother enveloped her daughter in her arms, smashing Evie's face against the beaded bodice of her

Weeping Woman wedding dress. "We'd lose you, Evie! Forever! I couldn't stand it! I couldn't! Don't do that to me, darling, say you won't! I—"

"OK, Mom," Evie mumbled, freeing herself from the hug. *"OK."*

Closing her eyes against Louise's smug grin, Evie called up an image of herself in the Spooky Little Girl outfit. When she opened her eyes and looked down, she was wearing the dreaded pink dress, the knee socks, and the pinchy black leather shoes. She couldn't see her hair, but she knew it was back to its usual fiery orangey red (to match Louise's). The ribbons drooped like lead weights on either side of her head.

Evie's mother cleared her throat. "Show me," she commanded.

Evie reached for Louise's hand. Standing side by side, they both fixed Evie's mother with identical haunted stares.

"Come and play with us," she and Louise said together in spooky singsong voices.

Evie's mother clapped. "Adorable," she declared. "*Frighteningly* adorable."

CHAPTER 3
WILLOW

There were muffled screams behind the closed door on the fourth floor. Several crashes. A sound like something heavy being dragged across the floor. Then an otherworldly, disembodied screech shook the hotel rafters.

But none of those things were what made Willow go suddenly pale.

"Oh no," she groaned.

"Oh yes," deadpanned Pierce, handing Willow the flyer that had arrived with the Hotel Ivan's morning mail.

"So Mr. Foster was right," Willow muttered.

"What are we going to do?" Pierce asked, and Willow blinked at his expression. If she didn't know better, she would have thought Pierce looked nervous. But Pierce was never nervous. He was never anything other than mildly annoyed.

Before she could answer, Pierce handed her another piece of paper.

"This came today as well. It says it's from the Truancy Board—"

Willow snatched the paper and crumpled it up. "That's a mistake."

"Hmmmm." Pierce gave her a look. "When was the last time you went to school?"

"I took a leave of absence," Willow informed him. "When Mom died."

"I wasn't aware you could take a leave of absence from sixth grade," Pierce countered, then softened his voice a smidge. "It's been six months now. Maybe it's time to think about—"

"A Hauntery, huh?" Willow said, changing the subject. "Why would they put a Hauntery here? So near us?"

"What are we going to do?" Pierce asked again.

"I don't know." Willow folded the flyer and tucked it safely into her back pocket. "But for now, whatever you do, please don't tell—"

"A HAUNTERY!" a voice on the other side of the door shrieked. "*A HAUNTERY!* This is the end! The ennnnnnnnnnnnnnnnnnnnd!"

Willow looked accusingly at Pierce, who shrugged.

"Leo got to the mail before me this morning. He was looking for his *Phantasm Weekly.*"

Willow took a bracing breath before opening the door. "Leo—" she tried, then promptly ducked as a china plate hit the doorframe above her head.

A rotund male ghost wearing a green velvet dressing gown over a black tuxedo floated by. Leo, the Ivan's Terrifying Phantasm, was a German-born former opera star with an undeniable flair for the dramatic. Between wails, he stuck two more dinner plates beneath his right arm, grabbed a serving tray, then took aim again. The tray shattered against a wardrobe on the far wall.

"*It's over!*" he bellowed. "There's no hope! None!"

He tossed another plate above his head, causing pieces of china to rain down from the ceiling.

"*Psssst!*"

Another ghost, this one wearing a dusty brown soldier's uniform, gestured frantically at Willow and Pierce from behind a chair. Willow could tell Alford was stressed. He always wore his death era outfit (that of a World War I American cavalry officer) when he was on duty haunting the second floor, but he only wore it during his off-hours when he was worried about something.

"Alford, what's gotten into him?" Willow asked as she and Pierce joined Leo's husband behind the chair.

"He's been like this all day," Alford said, kicking several pieces of a broken teacup away from where they were all crouching. "I don't know what brought it on."

"What brought it *on*?" Leo thundered, coming to a sudden stop in midair, causing his dressing gown to swirl dramatically behind him. "What brought it on? What brought it *ON*? I'll tell you what brought it on; my *voice*! My voice is *gone!* Gone, I say! It's gone!"

"All evidence to the contrary," Pierce pointed out, standing up with his hands protectively over his ears.

"Not my *normal* voice!" Leo snapped at the concierge. "My *Phantasm cry*. The very cry that the Vermont Board of Tourism called 'bone-chilling.' The cry that has landed me on the *Zagged Guide*'s Top Ten Phantasms in America list every year for the last eighty-five years!"

"Actually, you were number eleven last year," Pierce pointed out.

"CLOSE ENOUGH!" Leo thundered, throwing his last plate, Frisbee-style, at Pierce's head.

Pierce made a show of yawning as he leaned out of the way. The plate shattered against the wall behind him.

Now that Leo was out of ammunition, Willow stood up hesitantly.

"Surely it can't be that bad—" she ventured.

"Oh, really? You don't think so? Watch this."

Leo puffed out his chest and drew himself up so that he was floating several feet above the floor. A cold wind whistled through the room, ruffling Willow's hair. Leo raised his arms over his head, screwed up his face into a truly menacing sneer, and opened his mouth. Willow braced herself for his familiar earsplitting yowl (which, she knew from experience, the Vermont Board of Tourism had been absolutely right to call "bone-chilling")—but nothing came. Not even the tiniest squeak.

"See?" Leo floated back down to the floor with a hiccupy sob. "I don't know why I even bother. I might as well just Fade! Who would even notice? Who would even care?"

"Of course people would notice, honey," Alford said, coming out from behind the chair and taking Leo's hand fondly. "You're the Great Leopold! Your Fading, when it happens, will be an event for the ages. But it's not happening yet. Not yet."

"*I* would notice if you Faded, Leo," Willow added. "And I'd care. I'd care very deeply if you were no longer here."

Leo smiled wistfully at her.

"I probably wouldn't care," Pierce said unhelpfully,

ruining the moment and causing Leo to begin sobbing anew.

"Who am I kidding?" He paused to throw himself theatrically onto a chaise lounge. "It's already started. Look at *that.*"

Leo kicked off his bed slippers. Pierce gasped and covered his nose. Even Alford took a discreet step backward. But Willow, being Living and thus unbothered by ghostly foot odors, leaned forward and examined Leo's bare foot as closely as she could. She drew in a sharp breath when she saw that his big toe and the two beside it were missing. Gone. Faded. No doubt about it.

"Oh, Leo," Alford purred, fumbling around on the floor for the discarded slippers. He had the slightly congested-sounding speech of someone trying desperately not to breathe through his nose. "Let's get your slippers back on now—"

"No! I want her to see it! She *should* see it! It's her fault!"

Willow cringed at his words. Pierce stiffened. And Alford sighed.

"Now, now," Alford said disapprovingly, shooting Willow an apologetic look before he turned back to his husband. "She's doing the best she can—"

"Tell that to my Phantasm cry," Leo sniffed, ripping his slippers from Alford's hands and shoving them roughly back

onto his feet. "I may never get it back, have you thought of that? Then what? We'll lose guests. Without them and their fear, there's nothing to stop us all from Fading!"

Pierce snorted. "Somebody's been buying into the gossip again." He gestured to a nearby table, where, in addition to *Phantasm Weekly*, there were other crumpled magazines with headlines like "'Ghosts Require Fear to Remain on the Living Plane,' Says a Landmark Study by Professor J. Torrance" and "To Fear or To Fade: What the New Scientific Findings Mean for the Ghosts in Your Life."

"It's *science*," Leo snarled.

"One study." Pierce waved his hand in the air as though that could make it go away. "There's always some crackpot theory or another going around about Fading. People have been studying it for as long as there have been ghosts, and nobody's been able to figure it out yet. Why do some ghosts Fade right away while others stick around for centuries? Why do some people become ghosts in the first place while most don't? Nobody knows for sure. And probably nobody ever will. All of these so-called 'scientific' theories end up getting disproven eventually. It'll be the same with this one."

"What if it *isn't* a crackpot theory?" Leo argued. "What if this one's right? Can you think of a better explanation for what's happening to us? For what happened to Anna?"

"Oh, Anna's been Fading for decades," Pierce sniffed.

"Yes, but she didn't Move On until now," Leo pointed out. "Not enough guests means not enough fear. Not enough fear means *Fading*." He gestured to his now-slippered toes, then looked imploringly at Willow. "This is simply no way to treat the talent, my dear."

Pierce snorted. "And I suppose you think you're the talent in this scenario?"

"OF COURSE I AM!" Leo thundered. "As Leopold, I was the toast of Europe! Head tenor of the Hamburg State Opera. And as Leonata, I was a major off-Broadway star—the most sought-after drag performer east of the Mississippi. Alford and I only moved here for a little quiet, a change of pace—"

"And maybe it's time for another change, Leo," Alford cut in, taking Leo's hand again. "Maybe it's time for us to think about retirement."

"RETIREMENT?" Leo thundered, and Alford sighed, not looking entirely surprised at Leo's reaction. "Impossible! This hotel would crumble into chaos if I retired!"

"OK, Leo, OK. Have it your way." Alford held up his hands in surrender. "I'm sorry I brought it up. Let's just calm down . . ."

But Leo was in far too much of a state to do that.

"Every ghost in this hotel depends on me to generate

fear—including you, Pierce." He paused to glare at the concierge, who crossed his arms but didn't deny it. "Because of me, the rest of you can flit around, changing bed linens and taking our guests on themed excursions. I'm the Terrifying Phantasm! If I can't do my job, we'll all Fade. Me, my sweet Alford, all of us! *Doesn't anybody understand the pressure I'm under?!*"

With a loud sob, Leo threw himself back down on the chaise and slung an arm over his face. "And now a Hauntery!" he wailed into the crook of his elbow. "How can I possibly be expected to compete with that? We're doomed! Doomed, I say!"

"We're *not* doomed," Willow said quickly, with more conviction than she actually felt. A happy, confident staff was the key to a successful hotel. How many times had her mother told her that? No matter what her private feelings were, it was important that she instill confidence in everybody else. "Who cares about Haunteries?" she sniffed. "They're all part of a stupid, cold, corporate hotel chain—"

"—that owns three hundred and sixty-eight properties on four continents," Pierce added.

"—that doesn't know the first thing about true haunted hospitality—" Willow continued.

"—and that boasts a perfect five-star *Zagged* rating for ninety-five percent of its properties," Pierce concluded.

Willow glared at him. "The Hauntery ghosts get shuffled around between hotels so much, they never stay long enough to properly haunt a place," she pointed out. "We have *real* history here. We have warmth. Tradition. Guests can tell the difference. Guests can *feel* the difference. You'll see."

"But the Fosters—" Leo started.

"The Fosters were a fluke," Willow informed him, desperately trying to put aside the image of Mr. Foster, red-faced and bellowing, *Nothing here is scary!* "Even with the bad rating they left us, we still have a four-and-a-half star *Zagged* rating—that's plenty of happy, satisfied guests."

"So you're not at all worried about the Hauntery?" Alford asked.

"No, I'm not worried," Willow said defiantly, standing up as tall as she could. "My family has run the Hotel Ivan for four hundred years. We've survived wars, plagues, stock market crashes, and most of the staff dying. What's a stupid chain hotel compared to that? The Hauntery should be worried about *us*, not the other way around."

"But my voice!" Leo moaned.

"Rest your voice, Leo," Willow commanded, walking to the door. "Because we have a fully booked season coming up. Plenty of guests, which means plenty of fear to go around. We've got the Freeling family reunion coming in next week, then the Vermont Vapors next month—"

"The who?" Leo asked.

"The Vermont Vapors! You know, the soccer team? They've booked the whole hotel for a solid month. They'll be expecting the best, and we're going to give it to them. Because we are the Hotel Ivan! If anybody else on staff mentions the Hauntery, that's what you tell them!"

She opened the door, prepared to make a dramatic exit of which even Leo would have approved, before she remembered something and swung back around.

"Oh, and if anybody happens to see Molly's head, can you give it back to her? Thanks."

CHAPTER 4
EVIE

The magazine was a crumpled, faded gossip rag. The kind the Living liked to take on planes or on vacation. The type Evie was constantly finding strewn around the lobbies of every Hauntery she had ever haunted.

In addition to a teasing headline about Professor Torrance's new research on Fading, the cover featured a large picture of Kathleen Deetz, the founder and CEO of GhouledIn, a professional networking site exclusively for ghosts. The first-ever ghost billionaire.

The magazine wasn't the kind of thing Evie thought she would actually enjoy reading. It was a far cry from a Deena Morales Mystery—Evie's favorite series of books, which chronicled the adventures of brilliant teen detective Deena Morales. But that didn't matter. She stared at it anyway. She flexed her fingers once, then let them hover over the worn cover, directly above Kathleen Deetz's smiling face.

Evie lowered her hand slowly . . . then let out a loud, disappointed groan as her hand went right through the magazine (and the tabletop below) like a hot knife through butter.

"What are you doing?"

Evie jumped as Louise sauntered into the Hauntery lobby. Her cousin was still wearing the frilly pink dress from their Spooky Little Girl routine. Evie had changed back into jeans and a T-shirt the moment they'd gone off the clock. She couldn't stand the way the pink ruffles felt against her skin—the same kind of ruffles that were now swaying back and forth as Louise walked up to her.

"Were you trying to *touch* that magazine?"

"No."

"Liar."

"Go away, Louise."

Louise crossed her arms over her ruffles and sniffed. "You have to be a ghost for a long time before you can start manipulating objects in the Living world," she informed Evie, as though Evie weren't painfully aware of that fact. "You're barely five years dead. It takes most ghosts ten years at least."

Evie licked her lips. "I don't want to wait that long." She flexed her fingers, preparing to try again.

"You don't have a choice about it. It's the way things are."

Ignoring her cousin, Evie extended her hand over the magazine again, then dipped the very tip of one finger toward the cover. She willed herself to feel something. Anything. The remains of the slightly glossy finish, the feel of the paper crease that ran through the middle of Kathleen Deetz's forehead. *Something.*

But there was nothing. Evie felt only empty air.

Louise laughed. "Why not just try and touch a Living person while you're at it," she sneered.

"Don't be stupid," Evie growled at her. Not even the oldest ghost could touch a Living person. Nobody knew why. But almost every ghost got around to being able to touch non-Living objects eventually.

And if I practice enough, maybe I can do it sooner than most.

Louise rolled her eyes as though she had heard Evie's thoughts out loud. "Come on. Some test guests requested us on the third floor. Let's go."

"Play with us," Evie chorused in perfect broken harmony with Louise.

The couple at the other end of the hallway jumped. They were a middle-aged duo wearing matching *I Survived a Night in a Hauntery* T-shirts, which Evie thought was a bit presumptuous, given that Louise told her the couple had only checked in thirty minutes ago.

"Oh my!" the woman exclaimed, clutching the man's arm.

Louise tightened her grip on Evie's hand. Evie allowed herself to be dragged two feet closer to the couple.

"Play with us," they said again. "Please play with us."

"Oh, George!" The woman made a show of hiding her face in the man's shoulder. She had the look of smiley, shivery delight that people who enjoyed being scared often had in Haunteries. "How *ghastly*."

Evie, who couldn't have agreed more with the woman's assessment of the situation, was suddenly sure that she could endure this no longer. She squeezed Louise's hand twice; it was their agreed-upon signal that they should back away and end the encounter.

But Louise ignored her and dragged them a step closer.

"Come and join our game," Louise implored the couple.

"Um, well, I don't think . . ." George stumbled as his wife tittered with terrified glee.

Evie squeezed Louise's hand again. Again, Louise ignored her.

"We won't hurt you," she went on. "We know lots of games."

Evie took a breath. Even if Louise wasn't going to listen to her, she was going to end this one way or another.

Evie drew herself up to her full height the way she'd seen her father do before his act. She willed her face to change from the wide-eyed innocence of the Spooky Little Girl to the fearsome, angry expression of a Phantasm. She felt the temperature in the hallway drop. Wind whipped up around her. She rose several inches off the floor.

Louise, oblivious to her cousin's antics, continued on in an eerie singsong. "Play with us," she sang. "Play with us—"

"—FOREVER," Evie added in her best booming Phantasm voice.

It wasn't *quite* the roaring, thunderous cry her father had perfected, the one that shook buildings and sent chills down the spines of people blocks away. It wasn't even a cry at all—just a word, said in the spookiest voice she could summon. But it did echo up and down the hallway and cause a shock of icy wind to whip up the Living couple's hair.

The woman screamed. The man gave a strangled, frightened cry, and they bolted down the hallway toward the stairs.

Evie lowered herself back to the floor and turned

triumphantly to Louise. "Did you see that?" she squealed. "Did you *see* how scared they were?"

"What I *saw* was you breaking character," Louise said accusingly.

"Whatever. It worked. They were scared. Job done!"

"We're not supposed to scare them that way. That's the Phantasm's job."

"Who says?"

"Everybody says! Corporate. Our bosses. Your parents—"

"*Me.* I say."

Evie and Louise both froze as a very tall, very bald, very skinny man wearing a black suit walked down the hall toward them.

"Mr. Fox!" Louise called, running toward him. "I had no idea she was going to do that! I don't know what came over her. I—"

Mr. Fox put up a pale hand to stop her, then turned to Evie. "Ms. MacNeil, is it?"

"Yes, sir," Evie admitted. Mr. Fox, the vice president of quality control for the entire Hauntery Corporation, had arrived at the Mercer Street Hauntery just a day after Evie and her family. She couldn't help but think it was probably a bad sign that he already knew her name.

Mr. Fox narrowed his eyes at Evie. "Walk with me while I finish my rounds."

Without waiting for her to reply, he turned on his shiny heel and walked back the way from which he had come. Evie hurried to follow him after throwing a nasty look at Louise, who stuck her tongue out at her.

Mr. Fox led Evie down a stairwell, through a door, and into a cavernous underground kitchen. "Launching a business of this magnitude is an enormously complex undertaking," he informed Evie. "I don't expect you to understand most of it. What I do expect you to appreciate is that Corporate has sent me here to oversee the opening of this Hauntery location. And I will not be leaving until I'm satisfied that the entire staff is operating at or above the standards set out in the *Handbook*."

He paused to examine a stack of clean dishes, a tub of perfectly round melon balls, and a tray of cookies for that afternoon's Haunted Tea. He counted each cookie on the tray before nodding to a neatly uniformed ghost maid to take them away.

"Attention to detail is *vital*," he sniffed, then looked down his long nose at Evie. "And what I saw back there in the hallway was not a *Handbook*-approved guest encounter."

"I know," Evie admitted. "I'm sorry, but I—"

"Oh, hello, Mr. Fox! Hi, Evie!"

Patricia Spengler, the ghost who had complimented Evie's boots when she'd first arrived, appeared from around the corner. Patricia was the Hauntery's assistant baker, and Evie watched enviously as she picked up a tray loaded with muffins and held it up under the hotel manager's nose. Patricia had been only nineteen when she died, but that had been more than one hundred years ago, so now she could handle objects in the Living world as easily as anybody alive. Patricia was wearing the drab gray uniform that the kitchen staff was required to wear, and her hair was done up into an elaborate tower of black braids that made her just as tall as Mr. Fox.

Evie blinked. It was hard to tell for sure, but for a moment, it seemed as though the dark skin of Patricia's arm, the one that was holding the tray, became several degrees more translucent. But when Evie blinked again, the effect was gone, and Patricia's arm was no more see-through than that of any other ghost.

"Would you like a muffin, Mr. Fox?" Patricia asked. "I baked them fresh this morning."

Mr. Fox paused. "Are those blueberry?" When Patricia nodded enthusiastically, he shivered and wrinkled his nose. "I'm allergic."

"Really?" Evie couldn't help but ask. "I didn't know you could be allergic to those."

"My whole family is allergic to blueberries, Ms. Mac-Neil," Mr. Fox informed her icily.

Patricia hastily withdrew the tray.

Mr. Fox turned back to Evie. "Professionalism, Ms. MacNeil. That is the cornerstone of what we do. We are a Hauntery Hotel. Not some two-bit, family-run, fleabag bed-and-breakfast. Like that one nearby . . . uh, what do they call themselves, Ms. Spengler?"

"Do you mean the Hotel Ivan?" Patricia asked uncertainly. "That cute little place down the—" She cut herself off as Mr. Fox glared at her.

"*Cute* is an interesting word for that run-down old pile of bricks," Mr. Fox said, rolling his eyes. "Amazing that they have the audacity to even call themselves a hotel. Still, they're one of the oldest independent haunted establishments in the country. Which is why I'm here to personally see to it that they are *crushed into oblivion*. We'll show them how we do things at the Hauntery! We don't stand for mediocrity here."

Evie fidgeted uncomfortably at Mr. Fox's alarming tone. Patricia gave her a sympathetic smile before backing quietly around the corner with her tray.

"Mr. Fox," Evie began, "I know what I did wasn't, strictly speaking, part of the *Handbook*—"

"Strictly speaking?"

"Well, the *Handbook* does allow for *some* variation in our act. So I thought—"

"Let's see about that, shall we?" Mr. Fox pulled a well-worn, palm-size book from his back pocket. The cover read:

Official Hauntery Handbook

Employment Guidelines and Behavioral Expectations for

All Non-Corporeal Entities

38th Edition

Mr. Fox flipped through the pages for a moment, found what he was looking for, then cleared his throat loudly. "The roles of Spooky Little Girls will be played by two young female ghosts of similar height and build, dressed in identical, sweet, old-fashioned attire."

Mr. Fox paused to give Evie's outfit a critical look over the top of the book. Evie crossed her arms impatiently.

Hideous as it may be, she knew her dress was, at least, *Handbook*-approved.

"Spooky Little Girls will engage hotel guests and their children with friendly requests to 'play with us,' 'come and play,' or similar. These requests can be accompanied by smiles, giggles, and/or short pieces of adorable ad-lib dialogue."

He snapped the book shut with a loud thud. "Is any part of that job description unclear to you, Ms. MacNeil?"

"No, but—"

"And was there anything in that description about impersonating a Terrifying Phantasm?"

"No, but—"

"But what?"

"But they were *scared*, Mr. Fox. Isn't that the point?"

"The point, Ms. MacNeil, is that the job descriptions of contract ghosts have been set out in meticulous detail by Corporate. People who have more experience running a hotel than you. You are a contract employee, and you will fulfill the terms of your contract, and only the terms of your contract, or you will be replaced by another ghost who will. Is that clear?"

"Yes, Mr. Fox." Evie stared down at her shoes, hoping that would be the end of the matter. But Mr. Fox moved a step closer and lowered his voice.

"I'm aware that you and your family come as a package

deal. I'm also aware that yesterday evening, your father gave a Terrifying Phantasm performance that caused three of our test guests to faint and two others to be taken to the hospital with heart palpitations. Corporate was delighted. But even he can be replaced. One phone call to Corporate is all it would take to have new ghosts here tomorrow to replace you all in plenty of time for the grand opening. One more slipup, Ms. MacNeil, and I will make that phone call. Understood?"

"Understood," Evie echoed.

"I don't have to remind you that a bad reference from the Hauntery Corporation would make it virtually impossible for you or your family ever to find employment elsewhere?"

"No." Evie ground her teeth together. "You don't have to remind me."

Mr. Fox nodded and wiggled his fingers at her. Evie took this as a sign that she was dismissed and turned toward the kitchen door.

Ugh, Evie thought to herself. *The Living.*

"Smiles," Mr. Fox called after her. "Giggles. Short pieces of adorable ad-lib dialogue. That's your value to the Hauntery, Ms. MacNeil.

"Don't make us believe you're more trouble than you're worth."

CHAPTER 5
WILLOW

Willow couldn't remember the last time she'd worn jeans.

There was a strict business-casual dress code for the Hotel Ivan's staff. Willow owned four identical pairs of black wool pants with pressed creases down the front. Her mother had called them "slacks," and Willow always made sure to wear a pair when she was on duty. Which, lately, had been always. She hadn't even looked at a pair of jeans in . . . she couldn't remember how long. The pair she had on now was about an inch too short.

But they would have to do. Normal twelve-year-olds didn't wear slacks unless they were going somewhere fancy.

Willow pulled her curly brown hair back into a ponytail. She glanced in the mirror and flinched at the stark white complexion of the girl looking back at her. How long had it been since she'd left the hotel? She desperately needed some sun.

She flung a backpack over her shoulder and headed for the back door, hoping she'd be able to slip out unnoticed. Antonia, the Ivan's head chef, glanced up from the stove as Willow passed the kitchen, but she gave only a distracted wave before turning away to taste something that was bubbling on the stove.

With a sigh of relief, Willow put her hand on the doorknob.

"Where are you going?"

Willow jumped and turned around guiltily to face Pierce. "Nowhere."

"Is it school?" the concierge asked hopefully. "Are you going to school?"

"No," Willow admitted. "I'm going to the Hauntery."

"What?" Pierce looked very nearly startled—and for Pierce, that was saying something. He folded his arms disapprovingly. "I thought you weren't worried about the Hauntery."

"I'm not. I just . . . I thought I should see what we're up against. Just to be thorough."

"Thorough?"

"Yeah. Thorough."

"Hmmmm," Pierce said thoughtfully. "Well, hold on a moment. I'll ask Bree to cover the front desk so I can go with you."

"I can go by myself, Pierce. I don't need—"

"Go? Who's going somewhere?"

Willow turned as Leonata appeared dramatically in the hallway.

Leonata was Leo's drag alter ego. Unlike Leo, who was bald, barrel-shaped, and always looked rather somber in his stiff tuxedo, Leonata was a full-figured platinum blond who preferred bright colors. At the moment, she was wearing a neon-turquoise wrap dress with sky-high silver pumps (closed-toe, Willow noticed, to conceal her Faded toes) and a matching purse covered in tiny mirrors. Willow took a moment to marvel at her masterful makeup and long, talon-like red fingernails.

"I'm going to the Hauntery," Willow repeated. "It's not a big deal. I'll be back before you—"

"The Hauntery? Our *archnemesis?*" Leonata looked shocked, but she quickly recovered. "Are you spying? Is this a spy mission? If it is, count me in."

"We can't *all* go," Pierce reasoned. "Somebody needs to stay and run the place."

"Not It!" Leonata said, brushing by Pierce and moving to stand beside Willow. "Let the girls handle this one, Piercey."

"Aren't you supposed to be on vocal rest?" Willow demanded, trying not to choke on the thick cloud of Leonata's vanilla-scented perfume.

"This *is* vocal rest for me, sweetheart. I haven't rehearsed my Phantasm cry for forty-eight hours. And I won't do it now, either. Unless Pierce makes me mad."

Pierce just glowered at Leonata as Bree poked her head out of the nearest office, her Nikon swinging around her neck.

"Leonata! I need ten minutes later today—we still haven't done your portrait!" Bree's curly Afro was pulled into a puff on the top of her head today, and Willow spotted an EVERYTHING IS LOVE T-shirt peeking out from underneath her suit jacket.

"My portrait?" Leonata asked, sounding interested.

"For the 'Meet the Ghosts of the Ivan' series I'm doing on Instagram," Bree explained. "Everybody gets their own post, except you—you get two! See me when you get back, OK?"

Willow, who could see that her plan to escape the hotel unnoticed was already dead and buried, sighed heavily as Bree disappeared back inside the office. "Are you *sure* you want to go as Leonata?" she tried. "I don't want the Hauntery to know the Ivan's spying on them. I'm trying to be incognito."

"Well, I can't go as Leo—he's the number-ten Phantasm on the East Coast!"

"Eleven," Pierce corrected her.

Leonata waved him off impatiently. "Leo would be recognized immediately. Leonata is far more under the radar."

"Mm-hmm," Willow said, blinking at Leonata's bright dress as she held the door open for her. "Fine, let's go."

"The first Hauntery Hotel opened in 2010 in Arlington, Virginia. It was a modest establishment, boasting only twenty-six rooms and a staff of eighteen. Since then, the Hauntery has grown into a global corporation with three hundred and sixty-eight properties and counting . . ."

The stooped old ghost in the gray Hauntery uniform droned on, but Willow hardly heard him. Ever since she and Leonata had walked through the Hauntery's front gates beneath the fluttery sign that read GRAND OPENING: OPEN HOUSE, she'd had to work to keep her jaw off the floor.

She'd heard of Haunteries, of course. But none of what she'd heard nor the pictures she'd seen online had prepared her for the actual experience. The size of the building— there were ten times as many rooms as the Hotel Ivan! The sheer number of ghost employees. What did they all do?

Even the spooky music was weirdly effective. It was all pretty overwhelming.

And judging by Leonata's uncharacteristic silence, Willow guessed she felt similarly.

"The Hauntery's revolutionary business model," the guide continued, "which pairs a non-corporeal entity's—or NCE's—need to generate fear with a Living guest's desire to experience fear, has proven to be extremely effective. It has resulted in thousands of happy, loyal ghost employees and *tens of thousands* of satisfied Living guests worldwide."

Willow nodded politely to show the tour guide she was listening. She and Leonata were the only ones on this tour. There had been some confusion when they'd first arrived—everyone had assumed that Leonata was there to audition for a staff role. But once she told the stuffy manager that she was considering booking the Hauntery for an upcoming USO event, they'd been given their own private tour.

"It's not really a lie," Leonata whispered to Willow as their tour guide brought them through the lobby. "I used to be the USO coordinator for all functions concerning non-corporeal troops. It's how I met Alford—at a concert for deceased World War I veterans."

"Yeah, but you don't work for the USO anymore," Willow whispered back.

"Well, the Hauntery doesn't need to know that, do

they?" Leonata said with a conspiratorial wink before turning back to their guide. "Can you tell us a bit more about the property itself? My organization is only interested in booking *authentically* haunted locations."

"Of course, ma'am," the concierge simpered, gesturing around the opulent lobby. "The original building, as well as several of the building's ghost residents, dates back to the 1790s, just after the Revolutionary War."

"Wait, this building?" Willow asked, indicating the building they were currently standing in. "*This* building has been here since the 1700s?"

"Since 1790," the guide confirmed.

"I think there must be some mistake," Willow informed him. "I've lived on Mercer Street my whole life, and there's never been a huge building here before." For as long as Willow could remember, the property they were standing on had been a mostly empty lot with only a tiny defunct gas station on it.

"You probably just didn't notice it before," their guide said, looking nonplussed. "Our restoration team did a remarkable job returning the structure to its former glory, don't you think?"

"I really don't think I could have—" Willow began, but Leonata interrupted her.

"What's *remarkable*," she mused thoughtfully, "is that

there was a Victorian mansion in Vermont in the 1790s, decades before the actual Victorian era even began. Isn't history fascinating, Willow?"

"Oh, yes," Willow said, trying not to laugh.

Either the tour guide believed the nonsense he was required to recite, or he was very good at lying, because he continued on, straight-faced. "It's so important for business entities like the Hauntery to act as responsible custodians of our past," he continued. "Otherwise we'd be just another moneygrubbing corporation. And who needs another one of those?"

"Who indeed?" Leonata agreed heartily.

Their ghost guide continued talking as he led them past one of the two (two!) grand ballrooms. From there, they toured the 1920s-era tea parlor/cocktail lounge, the indoor swimming pool, the outdoor swimming pool—both with ghost lifeguards on duty at all times—and three spacious conference rooms with different themes: dungeon, mad scientist laboratory, and torture chamber.

Willow leaned in toward Leonata as they explored the torture chamber. "I don't get it. The Hauntery charges its guests about the same per night as the Hotel Ivan. How do they maintain all of this?"

"Not everything is as it appears, dumpling," Leonata replied with a meaningful nod toward a solid-looking chain hanging from the wall on Willow's right. Willow reached out a hand, readying herself for the touch of solid, cold metal.

Instead, her fingers brushed lightweight plastic. The chains were fake.

Which probably meant that everything else around them was fake, too.

"The Hauntery allows each guest to tailor their haunting experience to their taste," the guide droned on. "Whether you're a family on vacation looking for some lighthearted scares, a couple looking to spice things up with a serious fright, or a business leader looking for an unforgettable team-building experience, the Hauntery is ready to give you the time of your life."

The ghost guide paused in the doorway.

"You might say that we're just *dying* to meet you," he added drolly.

Leonata let out a rather stilted laugh, but Willow could only smile weakly.

"What about all of the employees?" she whispered to Leonata as several uniformed Hauntery staff members rushed by, flashing polite smiles that left their faces before they had a chance to reach their eyes. "How can they afford this many staff?"

"It's easy to hire four times the staff when you're only

paying them a quarter of what they deserve," Leonata said, and snorted.

The snort caused their guide to stop in his tracks. But Leonata gave him a winning smile, and he continued on down the corridor as though nothing had happened.

"Hauntery ghosts are paid peanuts," Leonata whispered to Willow as they passed a door marked HOTEL STAFF ONLY. "They only work here to avoid Fading."

"Because Hauntery ghosts never Fade," Willow mused.

"Exactly," Leonata said sadly.

The tour moved upstairs to a resplendent guest suite at least twice the size of the largest room in the Hotel Ivan. While Leonata distracted the guide with questions about the Hauntery's accommodations, Willow slipped around a corner and backtracked to the STAFF ONLY door. She nudged it open and peeked inside to find a barren, cheerless room. There was a large whiteboard on one wall that had "Employee Rankings" written above a long list of names. Willow could see only two categories: sufficient and insufficient. There was also a large picture of a scowling ghost above a sign that read, "Geoff van Gaff: Worldwide Hauntery Employee of the Month. No Vacation Days for Nine Years and Eighty-Seven Days (and counting!)"

Willow gulped and closed the door.

She caught up to Leonata and their guide just as they

were entering the (*award-winning!*) dining room, where Willow and Leonata were each given a tea cookie served by a vacant-eyed pastry chef.

"Does your restaurant have a Michelin star?" Willow asked as she chewed. The cookie was good—annoyingly good, actually—but it didn't hold a candle to Chef Antonia's famous melt-in-your-mouth butter cookies. Willow allowed herself to feel the tiniest bit smug. The Hotel Ivan's restaurant *did* have a Michelin star—the first Michelin star to ever be awarded to an establishment with a ghost head chef—and it was one of the hotel's proudest selling points.

"Michelin stars," the guide shook his head in disgust. "Those are a dime a dozen. Hauntery restaurants are staffed only by chefs who have won the James Beard Award. The World's 50 Best Restaurants Award had to change its name to the World's 75 Best Restaurants Award because there were so many Hauntery restaurants that qualified."

"Oh," said Willow.

"We constantly rotate our award-winning chefs through our properties so that our menus are continually updated," the guide continued. "At the Hauntery Hotels, we like to say that life and death are too short ever to experience the same meal twice!"

Willow exchanged a look with Leonata, and she could

tell they were both thinking about how many times Chef Antonia had served lasagna last week.

When the tour finally, mercifully came to an end, Willow followed Leonata outside and leaned against the (artfully) dilapidated back wall of the Hauntery for support.

"Well." Leonata tossed the business card the manager had given her in a nearby trash bin. "That was . . . interesting."

"It's worse than I thought it would be," Willow admitted. "The Hauntery makes so much money—they could afford to restore real old buildings and pay their staff fairly. Why don't they?"

"They're all about profit." Leonata tapped on the fake stone wall at their backs. "The more money they spend on the hotel, the less Corporate gets to keep. Real stone facades, fair wages—those don't come cheap."

"But don't the guests notice?"

"They don't seem to be complaining," Leonata said with a shrug. "This Hauntery isn't officially open, so it doesn't have a *Zagged* rating yet. But in a few weeks, it'll have a perfect five stars. They all do!"

Willow frowned. It just didn't add up. Of course the Hauntery Corporation wanted to make money; that was the point of any business, even the Ivan. But when Willow tried to imagine her parents lying to their guests about the Hotel Ivan's history or forcing the Ivan ghosts to give up their vacation days under pain of being ranked "insufficient" on a board somewhere, she just couldn't. The Ivan might be a bit shabbier around the edges than the glittering Hauntery, but that couldn't be what mattered most to the guests.

Could it?

"I'm glad we came," Willow said finally. "Now we know for certain that the Hauntery is as different from the Ivan as it could possibly be. People will figure that out. Won't they?"

"I hope so," Leonata said wistfully, not sounding nearly as certain as Willow wished she would.

They walked home in silence. When the Ivan, with its slightly crumbling brick facade, came into view, Leonata turned to Willow. "I've been meaning to talk to you about something."

"Oh?" Willow said distractedly. She was stuck on the tour guide's comment about *tens of thousands of delighted guests.*

"Your mom."

Willow stopped walking.

Leonata took a deep breath. "When someone dies and

then rises as a ghost, it's only natural for that someone's relatives to have, er, complicated feelings on the matter—"

"Complicated?"

"Yes." Leonata looked down and fiddled with the strap of her purse. "When your mom came back, we were all delighted, of course. And surprised. She's the first Ivan ever to come back as a ghost, did you know that?"

"Yes, I did."

"Of—of course you did," Leonata said hesitantly. "What I mean is, I know there was a lot of pressure on you to be thrilled to see her. And grateful to have her back in your life."

Willow squinted at Leonata, confused.

"What I'm trying to say," Leonata continued—Willow got the distinct impression that she was avoiding making eye contact—"is that it'd be okay if you weren't thrilled. Or grateful."

Willow stared at Leonata for a long moment before she swallowed and forced a laugh. "What are you talking about? She's my *mother*. Of course I'm thrilled I get to have another chance with her."

"I know you're happy she came back. I just mean you don't have to be excited about the *way* she came back . . ."

Willow fought back an image of her mother's last trip

down to the lobby. The way her mother had looked straight at her like she wasn't entirely sure who she was.

Willow?

"She's fine," Willow said dryly. "She's adjusting. It takes some ghosts a while, you know—"

"Yes, but it's been six months now. I think it's time to face the fact that she might be a—"

"Don't say it—"

"A WISP," Leonata finished.

Willow winced at the word, and Leonata sighed.

"I'm sorry, love. But somebody's got to mention it."

Willow drew in a breath. It wasn't at all rare for a recently risen ghost to be a little confused about what had happened to them. Most ghosts overcame this fogginess within a month or two and managed to settle into healthy afterlives until their eventual Fadings.

But there was a small fraction of ghosts who never managed to remember who they had been in life and who never quite came to terms with who they were now. The general rule was that if a ghost didn't adjust within a few months of their death, they were probably a WISP, which stood for "Woefully Impermanent Spiritual Presence." WISPs tended to Fade within a year or so.

Willow swallowed. "It's only been six months."

"I know, but—"

"She's still got time."

"Yes, but—"

"My mother is not a WISP!"

"Of course not, dumpling," Leonata relented, looking like she regretted bringing it up. "Forget I said anything. Should we go inside? I need to see Bree about my portrait."

Willow frowned down at her feet. "You go," she said. "I need some more air."

Leonata hesitated for a moment. She seemed to want to say more, but eventually she turned and walked into the Ivan without another word.

Willow watched Leonata's shiny turquoise dress disappear through the front door. But instead of following her inside, Willow kept walking.

And walking. And walking.

Walking felt better than thinking.

Thrilled. Grateful.

Willow shook her head to clear it of the thought.

Her mother was *fine*. It was way too soon to stress out about things like WISPs. They had much more serious things to worry about, like how they were going to make sure that the Freeling family didn't wish they'd booked their reunion at the Mercer Street Hauntery instead of the Ivan. No matter what Willow had said to Leonata about not being worried, she couldn't quite shake the memory of the

Hauntery's lavish lobby, that ornate guest suite, the swimming pools . . . She should really get back to the Ivan this minute and start working on a plan.

But for some reason, Willow didn't feel like going home yet. She kept walking until she reached the Mercer Street Public Library, whose doors opened automatically to welcome her inside.

CHAPTER 6
EVIE

It had taken Louise about three seconds to run to Evie's parents and report that Mr. Fox had witnessed Evie doing her illicit Phantasm act. It had taken Evie's parents about the same amount of time to confine Evie to her room so she could "think about what she'd done."

It had taken Evie significantly less time to decide that spending one more second in the Hauntery was thoroughly intolerable.

Smiles. Giggles. Short pieces of adorable ad-lib.

The snippets of Evie's job description chased her down Mercer Street. Every step she took away from the Hauntery was probably getting her into even worse trouble, but Evie didn't care. She might care later, but right now all that mattered was putting as much distance between herself and the ridiculous faux-Victorian knockoff as possible.

Maybe being fired by the Hauntery wouldn't be the worst thing ever. True, her parents would be angry, to say nothing of Louise. But she doubted Mr. Fox was right that they would never find work anywhere else. That couldn't be true, could it? And if they couldn't find work, how could they inspire enough fear to stay on this corporeal plane?

So what? Evie thought savagely. *What's the point of avoiding Fading when nobody really sees me anyway?*

She walked for a long time. She thought about how much she hated Mr. Fox. About how much she hated Louise. About how much she wished the dry leaves on the sidewalk would crunch under her feet. She walked until she eventually looked up and saw that she was standing in front of a large sign that said MERCER STREET PUBLIC LIBRARY.

Back when Evie was alive, libraries had been her refuge. Her safe place. She had been to even more libraries since her death. Every town the Hauntery Corporation had sent her to had a library—at least a small one. And Evie always found it.

But this time, it kind of felt like the library had found *her*.

Inside was the low hum of voices trying to be quiet, the comfortingly familiar smell of old books, and the glare of overheard fluorescent lights. Evie immediately felt calmer,

more herself, more alive than she had since . . . well, since she'd been alive. Everyone here was focused on their own business, and nobody paid Evie any mind. Which suited her fine.

She wandered until she found the travel section and lingered there. Maybe instead of Fading, she could travel. Preferably without Louise and her parents. Being on her own would be tricky, but she could manage. Once she learned how to move objects, anyway. Until then, traveling alone would be difficult.

If Louise was right, it would be years before that happened.

Disillusioned with the travel section, she wandered farther until she found herself in the children's section. She felt even more at home there, which was strange, when she really thought about it. Evie had been twelve when she died. But she'd been twelve for *five whole years* now, so shouldn't she feel older?

Evie never did. No matter how many years she spent as a ghost, she still felt and looked twelve.

The children's section was louder and rowdier than other areas of the library, and the shelves were messier. Evie looked around until she spotted a Living girl about her age, sitting in a high-backed armchair, legs folded beneath her, nose buried in a book.

But not just any book.

It was a Deena Morales Mystery novel.

Evie's breath caught in her throat. She walked very close to the girl with the book and looked at the cover. Mystery #11, *The Secret of the Ruby Dagger.*

Eleven? There had been only six Deena Morales Mysteries when she had died—had five new ones really come out since then? She'd stopped checking up on the series a few years ago. It was just too depressing to know that there were new Deena Morales books out there that she couldn't scoop up and read.

When Evie wandered away from the girl and over toward the correct shelf—*G* for the first letter of the author's name, Garcia—she saw that there were actually thirteen books now. *Seven* new novels had come out in the time she'd been a ghost!

The idea that her favorite teen detective had had seven adventures that Evie knew nothing about was almost physically painful. She felt a sudden intense longing to sit and read every single new book straight through without stopping. She could do it, too. One of the perks of being a ghost and needing no food or rest was that it greatly increased one's ability to binge read.

The problem, of course, was that there was no way she could even take the books off the shelf, let alone hold them while she read them.

Unless . . .

Evie crept back toward the girl, coming up behind her this time. A heightened ability to sneak was another upside of being a ghost. She was able to get right up behind the girl's elbow. When she peeked her head around the arm of the chair, she had a perfect view of Mystery #11.

The girl was starting chapter two.

Perfect. She hadn't missed much.

Evie passed the next hour happily ensconced in the world of Deena Morales. The Living girl read at about the same pace as Evie, which was convenient. She moved only twice, once to scratch her nose (almost losing her place) and another time to unfold and then refold her legs. That time she switched the book from her right hand to her left, but Evie simply moved so that she was looking over the left armrest instead and kept on reading.

It was bliss. Actual heaven on earth.

Until she heard a gruff voice behind her.

"Hey! What do you think you're doing?"

Deep in the book, where Deena was on the cusp of discovering the whereabouts of the missing ruby dagger, Evie was so startled that she stood up too fast. She tripped over her own feet and fell directly into the bookshelf behind her. Instinctively, she braced herself for a painful impact. But she didn't hit the bookshelf—she fell right through it, which caused the girl in the chair, the man who had startled her, and all of the children in the area to gasp.

"You're a ghost!" the man exclaimed. He was holding a squirming toddler and frowning down at Evie like she'd stolen something.

"Well, yeah . . ." Evie admitted, picking herself up.

"This is the *children's* section," the man informed her, shifting the toddler to his other side, farther away from Evie. "You don't belong here."

"I'm twelve," Evie pointed out.

"You're a *ghost*," the man repeated. "How dare you lurk around and scare innocent children!"

"She wasn't bothering me," the girl from the chair said pointedly. "She has every right to—"

"I was talking about my daughter," the man corrected her. "Not you."

Evie frowned. The toddler was squirming even harder in the man's arms and was starting to squawk like an angry bird. But it seemed to Evie that she was more annoyed about being held than frightened.

"If you ask me, public libraries shouldn't employ ghosts. They shouldn't even let them in the building!" The man sneered. "But in any event, they should keep them out of the children's section!"

"I was *reading*."

The man rolled his eyes. "Ghosts don't read."

"Of course we do!"

"Rubbish. You should be ashamed of yourself! Get out of here!"

"I told you, I was just—"

"*Get out of here!* Before I file a complaint with the police!"

Evie wasn't sure exactly what the police would (or could) do to her in this situation, but she didn't want to find out. She ran flat out, away from the kids' section, through the reference books, around the new releases, and out the door. She could feel tears on her cheeks. Ghost tears, of course. But they felt real enough to her.

She stopped when she got to the bottom of the library steps. She was back on the leaf-covered sidewalk, where the leaves refused to crunch under her feet.

I belong nowhere, she thought miserably. *Not in a Hauntery. Not in a library.*

I belong nowhere. And there is nowhere else I can go.

There was a sound behind Evie, and she turned, ready to run again.

It was the girl from the chair. She had the book they had been reading clutched tightly to her chest.

"I'm sorry about that guy," the girl said. "Some people are just idiots."

Evie felt herself relax a little bit. "Thanks for standing up for me."

"Don't mention it. Do you work here at the library?"

"Uh, yeah," Evie lied. It seemed easier than explaining that she'd run here because she was in trouble at her real job. A lot of older buildings hired ghosts just to hang out and help create a haunted atmosphere—it was a very popular starter career for ghosts who couldn't manipulate objects yet. Evie's attention drifted to the copy of Mystery #11 in the girl's arms.

The girl noticed her staring. "You like Deena Morales?"

"Yeah," Evie acknowledged. "My favorite is Mystery #4, *The Sign of the Witch*."

"Mine too!" The girl visibly perked up. "But for me, it's tied with Mystery #2, *The Clue in the Old Inn*. The one with the dinner party scene at the end—"

"The one with the poisoned wine goblet!" Evie interjected. "And the Medium!"

"Best ending *ever*!" the girl enthused.

"Totally," Evie agreed, then pointed to Mystery #11. "I haven't read the end of that one yet."

The girl held the book out toward Evie. "I've read this one before. I already checked it out, but you can take it if you want. As long as you return it on time. It's due two Tuesdays from now."

Evie licked her lips, walked up a couple of steps, and reached for the book. For a moment, she thought she felt her fingertips brush its crinkly plastic library binding. But when she squeezed her hand shut to grip the book, her fingers went right through it.

Evie dropped her hand and took a step backward. "I can't hold it by myself yet," she explained to the girl. "I'm a new ghost."

"Oh," the girl said, biting her lip and pulling the book back to her chest. "Maybe—"

There was a buzzing sound from the girl's pocket. She pulled out a cell phone and sighed at whatever she saw on the screen. "I should get home. I've been gone for way too long."

The girl walked past Evie, but then she turned and paused. "Maybe I could come back sometime, and we'll finish the book together. If you want?"

Evie was stunned. "Really?" she asked. "You wouldn't mind?"

"Not at all. Thursday? Four o'clock? Will you be working then?"

"I think so . . ." Evie hedged as she mentally reviewed her Hauntery schedule to make sure she'd be able to slip away again. "Yes, I can—I mean, yes, I'll be here on Thursday."

"I'll meet you at our chair." The girl smiled and turned to go.

"I'm Evie, by the way!" Evie called after her.

"I'm Willow!" the girl called over her shoulder. "See you Thursday!"

CHAPTER 7
WILLOW

For the next few days, Willow and the rest of the Ivan staff were so busy preparing for the Freeling family reunion that she hardly had time to think.

But when she did think, she thought about the girl from the library.

Willow didn't know exactly why she'd agreed to meet her again, except that it'd felt nice to be out of the hotel. And nice to talk to someone her own age. She hadn't done that since the last time she'd gone to school. That had been months ago. But talking to that girl—to Evie—it had felt like the old days. She could almost pretend that she'd stopped by the library after piano practice and that her mother was back at the Ivan, alive and waiting for her to come home.

But Willow didn't have much time to dwell on her new library friend. Not once the Freelings arrived.

It started out well. The family arrived on time, and check-in went smoothly. After a week of strict vocal rest and much fussing-over by Alford, Leo greeted the Freelings with a Phantasm cry that Willow was certain people must have been able to hear down the street at the Hauntery. After that, and after the smaller Freelings had been thoroughly delighted by Cuddles, the family was treated to a sumptuous dinner prepared by Chef Antonia. They all trotted off to bed, stuffed and excited for a week of ghostly family bonding.

But then came the next morning.

The adult Freelings were enjoying a morning horseback ride with Molly (who had found her head behind a milk crate in the attic), and the children were drinking hot chocolate in the lounge. With all the guests occupied, Willow hoped to use the time to change all the bed linens and tidy the rooms—but when she arrived at the linen closet, she found it empty.

"Didn't the linen service come this morning?" Willow asked Pierce. "Dad promised me he'd wake up to sign for it! I would have done it myself, but I was hiding the clues for the haunted treasure hunt—"

"He didn't get up in time," Pierce informed her, covering

the phone with his hand. "But it wouldn't have mattered. I have the linen service on the line, and they say they won't make any more deliveries until we've paid our outstanding balance."

"Our balance?" Willow asked.

"They say we haven't paid our bill in months."

Willow shook her head. "That's a mistake. Give me the phone, I'll talk to—"

A shriek from the kitchen made Willow jump. With an apologetic look at Pierce, she ran toward the sound.

"Francesca, what have you *done*?" Chef Antonia and her niece Francesca, the Ivan's sous chef, were glaring at each other over a steaming pot of pasta. A six-person film crew from Channel 13, the Mercer public access channel, stood awkwardly by as the star of one of their most popular shows, *Italian Classics with Chef Antonia*, violently stabbed a fork into the pot.

"I made it all exactly like you told me—" Francesca insisted.

Antonia speared a single penne noodle, dripping with red sauce, and popped it into her mouth.

"—except I subbed lentil pasta for the regular penne."

Antonia spat the noodle into the sink. *"Lentil?"* she sputtered.

"Cut!" shouted the director, a weary-looking woman with a very tight bun. "Chef, we really need a finished shot

of the pasta. Maybe you could try another bite and just *pretend* to like it?"

"Pretend?" Shaking with rage, Chef Antonia glared anew at Francesca. "This sauce recipe was handed down to me by your great-aunt Ginevra! She would roll over in her grave if she knew that her precious sauce was being poured over these . . . these . . ."

"Lentil noodles," Francesca supplied, rolling her eyes. "You didn't even really taste them, Aunt Antonia!"

Being ghosts, Francesca and Antonia didn't actually *need* to eat in order to sustain themselves. But, like all ghosts who had developed the ability to manipulate objects, they *could* technically ingest food when they wanted to. Most ghosts did this only on special occasions, as eating also required digesting and using the bathroom (which was a big hassle when you didn't do it regularly). Ghosts who worked in the food industry tended to eat more often, but they were usually pretty picky about what they put into their bodies.

Antonia grasped the pot by both handles. "I don't need to stick my head in a garbage can to know it stinks!"

"Aunt Antonia—*no!*" Francesca dove for the pot, but she was too late to stop her aunt from chucking the entire contents into the sink.

Antonia set the empty pot back on the counter with

a loud clang, which made Willow jump. "Out!" she whispered ominously to the film crew.

"But Chef, we don't have a finished show!" protested the director.

"We'll air a rerun this week."

"A rerun?" The director looked pale at the thought. "We can't just—"

"Out!" Chef Antonia thundered with such force that Willow wondered for a moment if she'd missed her calling as a Phantasm.

"Um, Chef—" Willow tried, sidestepping the film crew as they hurried to leave.

Antonia held up a hand. "We're all right in here, Willow. Lunch will be out momentarily."

Francesca shook her head and pointed to the mound of pasta in the sink. "That *was* lunch. I tried to tell you."

"I would never serve that filth in my dining room!" Antonia declared. "Lentil pasta? Who's ever heard of lentil pasta?"

"Nutritionists, that's who!" Francesca fired back. "Lentil noodles are full of protein! And flavor! Not like those tasteless regular noodles, full of empty carbs and—"

"Wait, *that* was lunch?" Willow gulped. The Freelings would be expecting a meal after they finished their ride with Molly. She looked frantically around the kitchen. "There must be something else we can serve, isn't there?"

But Francesca and Antonia didn't seem to hear her.

"Are you a nutritionist? Or are you a chef?" Antonia demanded.

"I'm both!" Francesca reminded her. "And you get emails all the time from viewers asking for healthy alternatives to your recipes. I love Great-Aunt Ginevra's sauce too, but what's the harm in pairing it with some new ingredients? Or using some new techniques—"

"She'd be *furious*, that's what's wrong!" Antonia threw a dishrag. "You have no respect for tradition!"

"And you're afraid to try anything new!"

"Maybe we could just do a salad?" Willow asked, dodging the bickering chefs and heading toward the fridge.

"Afraid?" Antonia looked affronted. "Do you think being 'afraid' is what earned this restaurant its Michelin star?"

Willow opened the fridge. Instead of a blast of cold air, she was immediately hit with the smell of rotting food.

"Do you think I became the first non-corporeal host in the history of public access television because I was *afraid*?"

Francesca rolled her eyes and looked up at the ceiling. "A recipe doesn't have to come from a dead relative in order to be good! That's all I'm saying!"

Willow cleared her throat. "*Guys!* What happened to all the food?"

Antonia and Francesca both looked at Willow as though they'd forgotten she was there.

"The fridge shorted out yesterday," Francesca answered. "Everything's spoiled."

Willow leaned her head against the (disturbingly warm) refrigerator door. "I'll call an electrician."

"I meant to tell you, Willow," Chef Antonia said, retrieving her thrown dishrag and using it to wipe her forehead. "But I kept forgetting. I haven't been myself lately. Not since I started Fading."

"Fading?" Willow exclaimed. "Not you too, Antonia!" She darted over and looked frantically at the chef's hands. They appeared solid. "Show me your feet!"

"No, Willow, my sweet," Antonia said gently. "It is not my body that is going but my mind. My brain, my talent. My very essence. There is more than one way to Fade, you see."

"That can't be right!" But when Willow looked around the nearly empty kitchen and thought about how much lasagna had been on the menu lately, it was hard to argue with the chef's logic.

Francesca took her aunt's hands in hers. "Why didn't you tell me?"

"I didn't want to worry you. You either, Willow." Antonia smiled kindly in Willow's direction, then turned back to her niece. "This is why we can't afford to waste time on silly nutrition fads. You must learn all I have to teach, and quickly. You must be ready. When I am gone, you must be the one to take over this kitchen. And my show."

Francesca's chin wobbled. Willow felt her eyes fill with tears.

Antonia dropped Francesca's hands and readjusted her chef's hat. "Pull it together, both of you. You're not to worry about me. Death is a part of life, and Fading is a part of death. All we need to worry about at the moment is what we're going to serve for lunch."

"I think there are some fish sticks in the freezer," Francesca said, wiping her nose. "I could fry some up on the stove?"

"Fish sticks it is," Willow said with a forced smile. "Yum."

Willow trudged back to the front desk. The thought that Leo and Antonia were both Fading felt like a lead weight on her back. She walked slowly through her favorite hallway on the first floor—the one lined with portraits of all the past Ivans. The first portrait was of Gracey Ivan, who had founded the Hotel Ivan more than four hundred years ago.

Willow looked up at her portrait.

Gracey Ivan had had a great swirl of silver hair, a heavily lined, no-nonsense face, and a slightly jutting chin that Willow recognized from looking in mirrors. The painting had obviously been done later in life, once the Ivan had already become a success, and Willow wondered what  Gracey had looked like when she was young. If only she'd come back as a ghost, she could have haunted the hotel and helped run it for all time.

But Gracey Ivan hadn't come back as a ghost. No Ivan ever had.

Not until Willow's mother.

"Do you have any advice, Gracey?" Willow whispered. "'Cause I could really use some."

Gracey Ivan remained silent.

Willow returned to the front desk and found Pierce on the phone again.

"Is that still the linen service? I can talk to them now—"

"It's not the linen service. It's the police."

"What?"

"The Freelings still haven't returned from their trail ride. I think Molly must have gotten lost. Three people have called the sheriff to report seeing them by the Overlook Mine. I'm trying to tell them we'll go retrieve them—"

"Yes! Please tell them that!" Willow ran a shaky hand over her curls, wondering how they could possibly get to Molly and the guests before the police did.

"I'm on hold," Pierce explained, then hesitated. "Have we really not been paying our bills?"

"My father said we were."

"We're not."

Bree came out of her office. Today, she was wearing a smart suit over a shirt that said THE FUTURE IS FEMALE, and her Afro was gathered into a side puff. She set one of the Ivan's accounting ledgers in front of Willow. "He didn't want to worry you," Bree explained. "But it's gotten pretty bad."

Willow closed her eyes briefly and wished people would worry less about worrying her. When she opened her eyes again, she blinked, trying to make sense of the dizzying columns of letters, vendor ID numbers, and bank names in the ledger.

"What's this?" she asked, pointing to the only column that seemed to have a positive number at the bottom.

"Oh, that's the Rainy Day Fund," Bree told her.

"The what?"

"Your parents set it up a long time ago, around when you were born," Bree said, closing the book abruptly. "Don't worry, nobody's allowed to touch the money in that account. I've made sure of that."

"But why—"

Pierce, still on hold, slapped a pile of envelopes down on the front desk. "The mail also came. There's another letter from the Truancy Board. And something from the *Zagged Guide*—"

Willow tossed the first letter in the bin and ripped open the second. "Dear Hotel Ivan Staff," she read aloud, "It's my duty to inform you that in light of the anticipated opening of the Mercer Street Hauntery, your designation as the number-one haunted hotel in your area has been temporarily revoked. *Revoked?*"

"That means taken away," Pierce explained.

"I know what it means!" Willow snapped, returning to the letter. "A *Zagged* hotel inspector will be dispatched shortly to conduct a detailed evaluation of both properties. They will then make a determination as to the definitive rankings of both hotels. You will be notified of the results in due course, and your entry in our official *Zagged* publication will be adjusted accordingly. Sincerely, Freddy Thompson, editor of the *Zagged Guide*."

Willow suddenly felt weak in the knees. "A hotel

inspector," she said feebly. "We've never had one of those before."

"What are we going to do?" Bree asked shakily.

Willow put the paper facedown on the desk and took a deep breath. "First we have to find Molly and the adult Freelings. Then I'll think of something to keep the kids occupied until their parents come—" She cut herself off as she spotted Alford walking by in full World War I uniform, gingerly leading one of the Freeling children up the stairs. "Alford! Where are you going?"

"I'm taking him to his room," Alford explained. "He's feeling sick. I think the milk in the hot chocolate may have been off . . ."

Willow shuddered, thinking of the warm refrigerator. Then she thought of something else. "Alford, if you're not watching the other kids, who is?"

"She said she'd look after them—"

"*She?*" Willow bolted from the lobby, ran around the corner to the music room, and skidded to a dead halt.

Her mother was standing in the middle of the room, right beside the piano. Her nightgown ballooned around her, fluttering as though she were standing in a breeze. A crowd of tiny Freeling children sat eagerly at her feet, paying her rapt attention.

"Are you really dead?" an intent boy with close-set black eyes asked eagerly.

Willow's mother nodded, staring over the child's head toward a patch of wall to the right of the doorway Willow was standing in. "Yes, I think so . . ."

"How did you die?" the same child pressed.

Willow's mother frowned. "I don't know."

The children groaned.

"Sure you do!" the same little brat shouted. "Come on, tell us!"

"I was checking in a guest," Willow's mother mused. "It was an ordinary day. Tuesday, I think. Wednesday, maybe . . ."

"Friday," Willow put in, unable to help herself. Seeing her mother here in *this* room, the room that had once been *their* room . . . Willow couldn't even look at the piano.

"Yes, Friday," Willow's mother said, although her eyes didn't focus on Willow. "I put them in room three. Queen bed with room for a rollaway. Nice couple. With a daughter. I had a daughter, too . . . I think I did . . ."

Willow's hands froze on either side of the doorway.

"Then what?" the child asked, leaning forward.

"Then I had a headache. A little headache. But sharp. Pierce told me to go lie down. I didn't want to . . . There was so much to do . . ."

Willow swallowed. She wanted to go. She wanted to stay. She wanted to kick the stupid kid who kept asking questions. But she was trapped in the doorway.

"The pain got worse . . . my head . . . such a sharp, sharp pain."

An aneurism. That's what the doctor at the hospital had called it.

"Then . . ."

"Then?" the boy repeated urgently.

"Then nothing."

"Nothing?" the boy repeated, and the crowd of children all drew back as one, disappointed.

"Nothing. Something. Then I was here, but not here. Here, but not—"

The boy made a loud retching sound and then bent double, throwing up into his lap. He was quickly joined by the two girls to his right, the older boy to his left, and then every other child in the huddle.

Willow's mother looked off into the distance, as though watching something of great importance. She slowly floated right through the piano and out through the back wall, seemingly unconcerned that her entire audience was now vomiting curdled hot chocolate and half-digested pancakes all over the floor of what had once been her favorite room in the hotel.

CHAPTER 8
EVIE

lick. Flick. Flick.

A guest had left a pen on one of the side tables in the lobby. Evie bent over it, flicking her forefinger over her thumb, aiming for the tip.

Back when she was Living, she'd spun pens without even thinking about it. But now, her finger kept going right through the stupid thing. No matter how many times she flicked, the pen refused to move. Until . . .

Ping.

The very tip of Evie's fingernail hit the cap, and the pen made a lazy counterclockwise circle on the desk.

Evie stared, not daring to look away as the pen spun around twice more, then stopped in the exact same position she'd found it in.

It *had* moved, hadn't it? She wasn't just seeing things because she wanted it so badly?

Evie bent down to try again.

"You're not even dressed," came Louise's accusing voice from behind her.

Evie looked over her shoulder at her cousin, then glanced pointedly down at her jeans and T-shirt.

"Really? I'm so confused. I thought these were clothes?"

"They're not your costume," Louise amended, folding her arms over her pink dress and snapping the heels of her shiny Mary Janes together.

"We don't have any hauntings scheduled until four. It's not even noon."

"You didn't read the new policy?"

When Evie shook her head, the corners of Louise's lips rose into a smirk.

"Mr. Fox posted it this morning. Didn't you see it in the break room? The policy says all Hauntery ghosts are expected to be in costume and in character at all times when on Hauntery property."

"But we *live* on Hauntery property," Evie protested, then felt her stomach drop. "Are you saying I have to be a Spooky Little Girl *all the time* now? We don't get any breaks when we can just be ourselves?"

Louise shrugged. "It doesn't bother me."

"Of course not," Evie muttered. Then she turned back to the pen.

"Ahem," Louise chided her.

Evie closed her eyes, bit her tongue, and reluctantly exchanged her jeans for the pink dress. Then she resumed her efforts at flicking the pen, trying not to imagine the satisfied grin on Louise's face as she walked away.

After another twenty minutes and countless flicks, Evie hadn't been able to make the pen spin a second time. But she didn't care.

I touched it. I know I did.

The thought brought her almost as much joy as the knowledge that there was a library full of Deena Morales novels just down the street. She was making progress. And even the *ohhhh*s and *ahhhh*s of some of the guests as they came out of the brunch room and spotted the Spooky Little Girl in the lobby couldn't dampen her spirits.

Evie could think of only one person at the Hauntery she could share her good news with. The only person nice enough, dead enough, and good enough at moving Living objects to help her take the next step.

Evie headed down to the kitchen.

"Has anybody seen Patricia?"

Two waiters heard her question but scooted away without answering. Evie could have sworn that one of them had red, swollen eyes, like he'd been crying.

"Patricia?" Evie tried again, this time to the line cook.

He shook his head sadly. "Sorry, Evie. Patricia's not here."

"Is she off today?"

"No . . ." The line cook set down his spatula. "Evie, Patricia isn't going to be around anymore."

"Why not?" Evie squeaked.

"She—" the line cook began, and Evie could have sworn *he* was about to cry. Then his eyes widened at something over Evie's shoulder, and he cleared his throat. "She's been transferred," the line cook said hurriedly.

"To another Hauntery property," added a familiar voice.

Evie turned to face Mr. Fox.

The cook snapped up his spatula and started busily scraping the grill.

"Transferred? Why?" Evie asked.

Mr. Fox shrugged. His bald head looked especially shiny this morning, and Evie briefly had the oddest thought that if she were to float up nose-to-nose with him, she would probably be able to see her reflection in Mr. Fox's pallid but polished forehead. "The Hauntery's Corporate headquarters often moves its non-corporeal assets from property to property when the need arises."

"Non-corporeal assets?" Evie repeated. The line cook shook his head slightly at her, but she ignored him. "Is that what we are to you? Things you can move around whenever you want?"

"Precisely, Ms. MacNeil. I'm glad we're starting to understand one another."

Mr. Fox grinned, picked up a cinnamon roll, then turned and swept out of the kitchen.

"The Living," Evie muttered at his back, eyeing an orange on the counter and dearly wishing she could throw it at him. But now that Patricia was gone, how was she ever going to learn to do that?

"You're looking for trouble there," the line cook said to Evie, pointing his spatula at her. "Best mind your business and not ask questions. Especially about ghosts being *transferred.*"

"Why? What happened to Patricia? Why shouldn't I ask about her?"

The cook shook his head. "Take some advice from an old ghost who's been around for a good while: Keep your head down, little Evie. And don't ask questions you don't really want to know the answers to."

***

Since there was nobody to practice moving objects with, no hauntings on her schedule until that afternoon, and an absurd new rule about what clothing she was allowed to wear on Hauntery property, Evie could think of nothing to do but go back to the library. It was only Monday, so she was surprised to find Willow sitting in the high-backed chair in the middle of the children's section.

"I thought we were meeting on Thursday?"

"We are," Willow said, and held up her book. It was Deena Morales Mystery #6, *The Phantom of Pine Street*. "I'm saving *The Secret of the Ruby Dagger* to read with you, but I couldn't wait until Thursday to come back here. I had a really bad day today."

"Me too," Evie said. "What happened to you?"

Willow put her book down. "We lost some guests. And we gave a bunch of others food poisoning."

"Guests?" Evie asked, not sure she'd heard her correctly.

"Oh, yeah, I work at a hotel. You know the Ivan?"

Evie swallowed and tried unsuccessfully to forget the time Mr. Fox had called the Ivan a two-bit, family-run, flea-bag bed-and-breakfast.

"I've heard of it," she said thinly.

"My family owns it," Willow continued. "I'm sort of in charge these days."

"That must be nice."

Willow snorted with laughter. "It's not as fun as you'd think. Especially on days like today."

"Did you find your guests?" Evie asked.

"Yeah. Our Headless Horsewoman eventually found her head and led everybody back to the hotel. But they all decided to check out the moment they got back. I'm not sure if it was because of the getting lost or the smell—"

"The smell?"

"From the vomit." Willow put her head in her hands. "There was *so much* vomit."

"Oh . . ." Evie wasn't sure what to say to that.

"They're probably all checking into the Hauntery right now," Willow added grimly.

"The—the Hauntery?"

"This fancy new hotel down the street." Willow raised her head and made a face. "You know the type—big, beautiful, but full of second-rate ghosts and greedy managers who only care about money? They're trying to put us out of business."

Evie, who couldn't help but bristle a bit at the "second-rate" comment, still found herself nodding sympathetically. "That's terrible."

"Yeah." Willow rubbed her nose, then shook her head to clear it. "But enough about me. What made your day so bad?"

"Um . . ." Evie thought fast. "My parents—it's like they both see me in this one way, you know? They won't let me do the job I want to do because they don't think I'm terrifying."

Willow bit her lower lip. "*Are* you terrifying?" she asked gently.

"*Yes,* "Evie said irritably, standing up straighter. "I mean, I know I'm not terrifying *right now.* But I can be. When I want to be."

"I'm sure you can," Willow said.

She had probably meant to sound encouraging, but Evie winced at the skepticism in her tone. She looked away, and as she did, she spotted a little boy halfway down the next aisle. He looked about eight years old, and he was ripping the title page out of a book.

"I'm sick of being treated like a little kid," Evie went on. *Little Evie,* she thought to herself as the boy crumpled up the piece of paper and tossed it onto the ground. *Smiles. Giggles.* She looked away from the boy, toward the book in Willow's lap. "Nobody ever treats Deena Morales like a little kid."

"True, but she's Deena Morales. You and I are just . . .

us," Willow said wistfully. Then they both flinched as the boy noisily ripped another page out of the book.

Evie motioned to Willow to wait a moment. Ducking around Willow's chair, she crept up the aisle behind the boy. He was too busy ripping out pages to notice her. She closed her eyes for a moment, then hovered just behind him with her head over his right shoulder.

"QUIT. IT," she growled in her best Phantasm voice.

The boy jumped. The ruined book tumbled to the floor as he bolted down the aisle, straight out of the children's section.

Evie tried to look nonchalant as she walked back to the chair.

"Not bad," Willow said approvingly.

"It's a work in progress," Evie said with a shrug. "My Phantasm cry is still sort of . . . developing."

"Oh, you'll get there." Willow's voice was now entirely encouraging, without the skepticism from earlier. "If we had a job opening for a Phantasm, I'd hire you in a second."

"Really?" Evie asked, unable to stop the warm and fuzzy feeling that flooded her at Willow's words. A job offer, sort of. And not for the job of Spooky Little Girl—for a Phantasm!

"Sure. Except we already have a Phantasm. And we don't have any extra money right now." Willow's face darkened.

"And I don't think you'd really want to work for me. Not when we might have to close down."

"Oh." The warm fuzzies faded into sympathy at the sight of Willow's face. "You really might go out of business?"

Willow shrugged. "I hope not. The Hotel Ivan's been in my family for four hundred years—I really don't want to be the Ivan who loses it. Ugh, that *stupid* Hauntery!"

"Yeah . . . stupid Hauntery," Evie repeated with a guilty lump in her throat. "Hey, you know—"

Willow's phone buzzed. When she retrieved it, Evie could see several missed texts on the screen.

"I have to go," Willow said, standing up quickly from the chair.

"Willow?"

"Yeah?"

Evie drew in a breath. "The Hauntery isn't that great. I mean—I don't know much about it," she added hastily. "But it can't be as amazing as everybody thinks. You shouldn't give up on your hotel." She pointed to Mystery #6, which Willow was still holding. "Deena Morales wouldn't give up."

A thoughtful smile spread across Willow's face.

"You're right. She wouldn't."

CHAPTER 9
WILLOW

The hotel was eerily silent when Willow jogged into the empty lobby. She expected to find Pierce, who had just sent her an eighth text, waiting for her. But instead, she found her father. He was sitting all alone on one of the red couches. When he spotted Willow, he blinked.

"Where were you?" he asked.

"The library," Willow answered. Then she caught sight of her father's slippered feet on the coffee table and found herself suddenly shaky with rage. "Where were *you*?"

"Where was I when?"

"Oh, I don't know." Willow ticked off the possibilities on her fingers. "This morning, when you were supposed to sign for the linen delivery? This afternoon, when the police were here? Or when I was scrubbing vomit off the floor of the music room? Any time in between? Take your pick, Dad!"

"I'm sorry, Willow, I haven't quite been myself since . . . since . . ."

"Since Mom died. You haven't been yourself since Mom died. You haven't been *anybody* since Mom died!"

He lowered his face into his hands. "I'm sorry," he muttered. "You've been doing it all, I know. You've been doing an amazing job."

Willow laughed bitterly at that. She laughed so hard she snorted. "No, I haven't! I'm *drowning* here!" Her voice reached a hysterical pitch she barely recognized as her phone buzzed again. "I needed you today. I need you every day. Don't you get it? *I can't do this by myself!*"

"I know," her father groaned into his hands. "I know."

"I made you an appointment with Dr. Strode. Two appointments! You missed them both."

"I know. I'll go to the next one. I promise, Willow. I'll go."

There was a long silence.

"How long haven't we been paying our bills?" Willow asked finally.

He looked up at that. "A couple of months. Maybe three."

"Why didn't you tell me? And *don't* say you didn't want to worry me."

Her father scratched his head. "It's not as bad as it seems. If we can hold out until the Vermont Vapors get here, we'll be all right. After they pay us for an entire month, we can pay everybody else. I was trying to get us by until then."

"What about the Rainy Day Fund?"

"How do you know about—"

"Bree told me. What's the Rainy Day Fund?"

Willow's father frowned. "We can't use that."

"Why?"

"That money is not for the hotel."

"What do you mean? Why can't we use—"

"That money is for you, Willow."

"Me?" Willow squeaked, and her father sighed.

"Your mother and I saved it for you. So that if the hotel went under, or if anything happened to us, you'd be provided for. It's not for just any rainy day, it's for *the* rainy day. When there's nothing else left. Your mother wouldn't have wanted us to spend that."

Willow snorted again. "Yeah, well, I can think of a lot of things that Mom wouldn't have wanted."

"Willow—"

"I'm losing them, Dad! Leo, Antonia, all of them! I'm losing *her.* They're Fading. If I can't think of something, we're going to lose them all. We're going to lose Mom all over again! *Help me!"*

Over her father's shoulder, Willow saw Pierce poke his head into the lobby.

"Willow? There you are. I've been texting you."

"Sorry, I got—"

"You'd better come. It's Leo."

"Leo?" Willow's heart jumped into her throat as she rushed to follow Pierce through the door that led to the staff quarters.

"I'll do better," her father said from the couch. "I promise. I'll do better."

Willow let the door slam behind her.

Leo and Alford's room was packed. Pierce and Willow joined Molly and Antonia against the back wall. Francesca and Bree were crammed in front of a bookshelf in the corner.

Leo lay prostrate on his chaise lounge in the center of the room with Alford kneeling at his side and Cuddles snuggled up against his legs. It seemed to Willow that Leo was wrapped in his finest dressing gown, but it was hard to tell. You had to squint to see him, and there were times when his body seemed to flicker in and out of sight.

Willow was aghast. "He seemed fine this morning when

he did the Phantasm cry," she whispered to Pierce. "How did he get so bad so quickly?"

"It must have been his Last Gasp," Pierce answered, also in a whisper. "His last burst of energy before he Moves On."

Alford looked back over his shoulder. "He wanted to do one last show. He wouldn't let me tell anyone—" Alford cut himself off with a sob.

Leo reached over and felt for his husband's hands. "Don't cry, Alfy. Not now."

Alford chuckled. "If not now, at the end, then when should I cry?"

Leo shook his head. "No crying," he said firmly. "Not after we've had such a glorious death together."

"We did," Alford agreed, wiping tears from his mustache. "We really, really did."

"I'm sorry we never retired," Leo said. "It's my fault—"

"Don't worry about that, Leo," Alford assured him. "I wouldn't change a thing. Really."

Willow heard Pierce draw in a deep breath before he took a step forward. "Leo?"

"Pierce? Is that Pierce?"

"Yes, Leo. I told you once that I wouldn't miss you if you Faded."

"Yes, you did."

Another deep breath. "I was wrong about that."

"Thanks, Pierce."

The concierge backed up again to stand beside Willow. His shoulders were shaking.

"No crying!" Leo bellowed, trying to sit up but coughing loudly before falling back on the chaise lounge. He was almost entirely transparent now, so much that he was nearly invisible, and there was not as much time between flickers.

"I'm sorry, Leo," Willow said quietly, starting toward him. "I'm *so* sorry—"

"This isn't your fault, dumpling." Leo raised his head to look at her, and for a moment, Willow could have sworn she saw Leonata's makeup and platinum-blond hair in the next flicker. She winked at Willow, then flickered back to Leo's stubbly features. "I won't have you thinking that. And I won't have you stealing my death scene, either. So back up, love."

Willow let out a watery chuckle and took a step backward.

Leo blew her a kiss, then fell back onto the cushion with a frown. "I'm ready. I'm ready to go. But I don't know how. I don't know . . ."

"Don't know what, Leo?" Alford asked.

"I don't know what to do," Leo said, his forehead creased in frustration. "They're all here. Everyone is here, and I don't know what I'm supposed to do."

"You're not *supposed* to do anything, honey—"

"I want to do something! I need to do something!"

Everyone was silent for a moment, until Alford suddenly sat up straighter. "Sing," he said.

"Sing?" Leo asked, sounding doubtful. But Alford was standing up now and pulling Leo to his feet.

"Like the old days, honey. In the opera houses. You remember."

"The opera houses . . ." Leo murmured, standing none too steadily. Alford put his arms around Leo to steady him, and Willow blinked. Alford had started to flicker too. His brown uniform was growing hazier by the minute.

"The stadiums, the theaters," Alford said into Leo's ear. "The Palais Garnier—the USO show where we met, remember?"

"I remember."

"Row upon row of those beautiful red velvet seats," Alford murmured. It was so quiet in the room that everybody who was assembled could hear him, too. "The instruments, the costumes. You standing center stage. Singing to a packed house. The aria—"

"The aria . . ." Leo smiled.

"Sing, my love," Alford whispered. "One last time."

Leo drew himself up on his almost-invisible legs. His voice filled the room. Not his Phantasm cry, the one that had shaken the rafters and haunted the rooms of the Hotel Ivan for so long. Instead, the room quivered with a beautiful, reverberating tenor that shook the tears out of everyone present in spite of Leo's command that they should not cry.

The aria came to an end. Only Leo's outline was visible now. He kissed Alford, and then his eyes drifted up toward something near the ceiling.

"Alfy," he rasped. "Alfy . . ."

Then he Faded from sight, dressing gown and all, leaving Alford with his arms wrapped around nothing but air.

"Wait for me," Alford said softly. "Wait for me, Leopold. I'm coming."

He closed his eyes, breathed out once, and he, too, was gone.

Alone on the chaise lounge, Cuddles buried his face in his paws and cried.

Willow hung up the phone.

"Well?" Pierce asked.

"That was the Vermont Vapors."

"And?"

"They're canceling their stay with us. The entire month." The words felt heavy in her mouth. "It seems the Hauntery offered them a better deal."

Pierce looked down at the floor. "So that's it, then. We're finished. The Hauntery's won."

Willow took a deep breath. Agreeing with him would be awful, but it would also be a relief.

But then, for some reason, Willow thought about something Evie had said in the library.

You shouldn't give up on your hotel . . . Deena Morales wouldn't give up.

Slowly, Willow pulled out the *Zagged Guide*'s letter. "Not yet," she said. "They haven't won yet."

Pierce shook his head. "Willow, I know what you're thinking, but—"

"But what, Pierce? Things are bad right now, I know. But what if we can get that inspector to rank us number one? We'll get our guests back! Nobody else will Fade. We still have a chance."

"But how can we possibly—"

"We weren't trying hard enough before. That's my fault. I told everybody that the Hauntery didn't matter, that we shouldn't worry. I was wrong. I see that. And now we're going to beat them at their own game."

Pierce raised an eyebrow.

"We'll be better," Willow continued. "We'll be scarier. We'll fix this place up to be the scariest haunted hotel anybody has ever seen. Way scarier than any cookie-cutter Hauntery."

"With what money? We can't even pay our bills! We need to fix the fridge and pay the linen service . . ." Pierce trailed off and lowered his voice. "If you need a loan, Willow, I'd be more than happy to—why on earth are you smiling?"

Willow *was* smiling. She was also looking out the window, out at the clear blue sky.

"I don't need a loan, Pierce. I feel a rainy day coming on. How about you?"

That evening, Willow tacked a note to the message board at the Mercer Street Public Library.

To Evie, the library ghost:

If you see this note before
we meet on Thursday,
please come to the Hotel Ivan.
I'd like to offer you the position
of Terrifying Phantasm.

—Willow

CHAPTER 10
EVIE

W*hat* are you wearing?" Evie asked.

Louise spun around, running her hands over the lapels of her new black suit. It looked exactly like the suit Mr. Fox always wore.

Which, Evie was pretty sure, was the point.

"I got it!" Louise announced, her eyes sparkling.

"Got what?"

"The internship!"

Evie stared at her blankly.

"You know, the management internship with Mr. Fox?"

"Oh, right."

Last week, Mr. Fox had made an announcement about taking applications for an internship, which he had called "an exciting advancement opportunity." Evie vividly

remembered wondering who on earth, alive or dead, would voluntarily sign up to spend more time with Mr. Fox than was absolutely necessary.

Apparently, she had her answer.

"Kathleen Deetz started out in hotel management, you know," Louise informed Evie. "Before she started GhouledIn."

"Oh, so now you think you're going to become a millionaire like her?"

"She's a *billionaire*. And who knows? Maybe I will. I'm not going to be a Spooky Little Girl forever. Mr. Fox says I have *management potential*. You should really start thinking about your future, too."

"I'll get right on that."

"I'm serious. It's about time you stopped this nonsense about wanting to be a Phantasm and started setting some realistic goals for yourself."

"Like being a billionaire?" Evie scoffed.

Louise stuck her nose in the air. "At least I have my sights aimed high. As far as I can tell, you aren't aiming at *anything*."

Evie gritted her teeth, then remembered the note she'd seen on the message board at the library that morning. What she wouldn't give to tell Louise that she had a job offer—as a Terrifying Phantasm! If she didn't know for an absolute fact that Louise would run straight to Mr. Fox with the news, she'd tell her right this minute. The look on Louise's face would almost be worth getting fired . . .

Almost. But not quite.

"Your parents think the same thing," Louise continued. "They were talking to me about it before they left."

Evie's mom and dad had been loaned out to Phamazon for the next few days. Phamazon, the Hauntery's sister corporation, was the largest online retailer of non-corporeal-entity-related products in the world. In addition to its exclusive line of Hauntery memorabilia, which included everything from mugs to T-shirts to reusable grocery bags, Phamazon also rented out Hauntery ghosts for private events. Some rich person from Florida had hired Evie's parents via Phamazon to haunt their vacation house in Boca Raton for the weekend.

As far as Evie was concerned, the trip couldn't have come at a better time.

"Your parents are as worried about your prospects as I am," Louise went on. "They won't say it to your face because they don't want to hurt your feelings."

"Well, aren't I lucky that you don't worry about things like that."

"There's no place for feelings in the business world," Louise said sagely, turning toward the door. "I'm shadowing Mr. Fox this afternoon. What are *you* doing?"

Evie shrugged and faked a yawn. "Oh, I'm sure I'll think of something . . ."

When Evie walked through the open front door of the Ivan, she hardly had time to look around before a small white blur came streaking toward her, followed by a woman holding a camera.

"Catch him! Catch him!" the woman yelled.

Evie reached down and seized the blur right before it managed to run between her legs and out the door. She did it without thinking and was briefly elated that she had managed to *touch* something Living. But upon closer inspection, it became clear that the white blur was actually a ghost—a ghost *dog*, Evie realized as a tongue appeared from somewhere in the depths of the fuzz and gave her a very thorough face-licking.

"Sorry!" The woman with the camera scooped the creature out of Evie's arms. "I'm trying to take his picture by the front desk, but he just won't stay put!"

"No wonder," said a sharply dressed man behind the front desk, who was wrinkling his nose in disgust. "He had another accident back here."

"Cuddles!" the woman with the camera admonished the fluff ball. "Not again!"

"I *knew* I smelled something," said a second woman on the other side of the lobby. This woman was headless and walked right into a standing lamp.

Evie took a quick second to look around. To someone used to the grandeur of Hauntery lobbies, the Hotel Ivan's lobby was kind of a letdown. It was all a bit dark and shabby, with peeling wallpaper, old furniture, and a layer of dust on everything. But still, with the cozy fireplace and the assorted knickknacks on every surface, Evie thought the Ivan looked very homey.

It reminded her of something she couldn't quite put her finger on.

"It's not Cuddles's fault," the man behind the desk was saying. "This happens every time he eats anything besides the Good Ghouls treats. Who's been giving him Living food?"

"Maybe it was a guest?" the headless woman ventured.

"We don't have any guests!" the man thundered back.

The fluff ball made a tiny whining sound. The woman holding him set him back down on the ground, and he scuttled away, looking vaguely ashamed as he wove between the ankles of the two women in chef's hats who had just entered the room.

"I think Cuddles is Fading," announced the older of the two chefs. "He's forgotten his obedience training,"

"Molly, look out!" the younger chef yelled, then darted over to steady the headless woman, who had just blundered straight into a bookcase.

"I'm so sorry about all of this," the woman with the camera said, drawing Evie's attention back to her. "How can we help you?"

"Are you a guest?" asked the headless woman, sounding hopeful, as the young chef guided her over to a couch. The sharply dressed man had produced a pooper scooper and was dealing with the mess behind the desk.

"Er, no," Evie started. "I'm here for—"

"Pierce, can Living guests smell ghost poop?" the younger chef asked.

"I don't think so," the dour-looking man answered.

"*So sorry,*" the camera woman said to Evie again, shooting a severe look at the rest of the ghosts in the room. "You were saying?"

But just then, Willow came into the lobby. "Pierce, I think Cuddles may have stolen my sandwich. Have you—" She stopped, catching sight of Evie. "You're here! Does this mean you're accepting the job?"

"Job?" The sour-faced man—Pierce, Evie supposed— suddenly stood up straight, pooper scooper still in hand. "What job?"

Willow gestured grandly toward Evie. "Everyone, this is Evie. I've offered her the job of Terrifying Phantasm."

"You—you—" Pierce stammered. He turned toward Evie and looked her severely up and down before turning back to Willow. "Her? *She's* the new Phantasm?"

"*Yes,*" Evie said, her whole body prickling with annoyance.

"You can't just go around hiring people," Pierce complained to Willow. "For one thing, the Ivan doesn't have the money—"

"Yes, we do," Willow corrected him. "There's the Rainy Day Fund, remember? I used that."

"How?" Pierce demanded. "You're twelve! Who authorized—"

He cut himself off as his eyes slid accusingly toward the woman holding the camera.

"It's her money," the woman said with a shrug. "And anyway, it's not like she wanted it so she could go shopping, Pierce. She's trying to help."

Pierce sighed and looked away. Evie could have sworn she saw the camera woman wink at Willow behind his back.

"The Ivan's not the Ivan without a Terrifying Phantasm," Willow said as she turned to Evie. "You're definitely taking the job, right?"

"Sure," Evie said, looking around uneasily. She'd really envisioned having this conversation with Willow in private. "I need to talk to you about my other job, though . . ."

"The one at the library?"

"Um, yeah . . ." Evie bit her lip and thought fast. She couldn't very well tell an entire lobby full of ghosts from the Ivan that she actually worked at a Hauntery—and as a Spooky Little Girl, no less.

Not now, at least. Not until she got to know everybody.

"I have to keep my, er, other job, too," she said finally. "For personal reasons."

Willow looked relieved. "Oh, that's fine," she said. "We scheduled our last Phantasm's hauntings around his drag show schedule. We can schedule yours around your library duties."

"Great!" Evie said, looking around the room at her new coworkers. The two chefs looked only mildly interested in what was going on. The headless woman—Headless *Horse*-woman, Evie corrected herself, noticing her spurs—wasn't really looking anywhere, due to her lack of eyes. Pierce was still glowering at her.

Only the woman with the camera was giving her anything close to a welcoming smile.

"Now that we're all here," Willow said, "I officially call this staff meeting to order. I was hoping my father would be able to make it," she added, glancing at her phone, "but he must have forgotten. You can meet him later, Evie."

Evie nodded. Willow quickly introduced the rest of the Hotel Ivan staff to Evie by name, then cleared her throat importantly.

"I got an email from the *Zagged Guide* this morning," she announced. "They said that their hotel inspector, a Mr. Renard, will be arriving here in four days to look over the Ivan. He'll be spending the night at the Hauntery the day before."

"Why does the Hauntery get to go first?" the Headless Horsewoman—Molly—complained.

Willow shrugged. "I don't know, but it doesn't matter. This is our last chance. We have to get that inspector to give us back our number-one spot, or . . ." She trailed off, then cleared her throat loudly. "So we have four days to come up with a plan. Anybody have any ideas?"

There was a deafening silence.

"Anybody?" Willow asked hopefully.

"Maybe we could spiff up the lobby a bit?" Francesca, the younger of the two chefs, suggested.

"I could pull the good china out of the attic," Pierce added.

"And *I* will almost certainly find my head by then," Molly offered.

"Good, all good," Willow said. Evie thought she was trying very hard to sound encouraging, but it ended up coming out a bit sad.

"Francesca and I will come up with a *fantastic* menu," the elder chef, Antonia, promised. "We'll stuff that inspector so full of delicious meals, he won't know what hit him!"

"Good!" Willow said, a tad more enthusiastically. "Food is good. Maybe that will be enough. Between good food and nice china and the, er, the spiffing . . . maybe that will be enough."

"I'm sorry," Evie said before she could stop herself, "but no, it won't be."

Every eye in the room came to rest on her.

"How can you know that?" Pierce asked. "You've been here what, five minutes?"

"I know what Haunteries are like!" Evie countered, then bit her lip. "I mean, I—I stayed in one once. The guest spaces are nice. Like, super over-the-top nice. They have ballrooms and swimming pools and a million ghosts on staff—"

"Are you saying the Ivan isn't 'nice'?" Pierce growled accusingly.

"We *are* down to a three-point-two *Zagged* rating," Molly admitted. "The Mercer Street Hauntery has a perfect five. I checked this morning. Before I misplaced my head."

"The Hauntery shouldn't have a perfect rating," Willow said. "After Leo and I visited, we gave them a bad review. Has it not shown up on the site yet? That's strange . . ."

"The Ivan *is* very nice," Evie said. She looked around the lobby again, which, she had to admit, could definitely use some spiffing. And which definitely still reminded her of something. "It's homey in here. Friendly. Inviting. It's the kind of place you can relax in. Haunteries aren't like that."

"So what are you saying?" Pierce asked impatiently.

The woman with the camera—Bree—stepped forward. "I think what she's saying," she interjected with a nod toward Evie, "is that we're not going to beat the Hauntery at its own game. We're never going to be fancier or more luxurious, no matter how much we spiff. And I agree. Evie's saying we should do what *we're* good at. Right, Evie?"

"Right," Evie said, smiling gratefully at her.

"What *we're* good at . . ." Willow mused. "I guess we're good at making people feel comfortable? Giving them a good experience?"

"We *were* good at that," Molly said sourly, "until recently."

"We're *still* good at that," Willow insisted. "But how do

we show the inspector that? How do we make sure he has a once-in-a-lifetime experience here?"

At that exact moment, Evie realized what the Ivan's lobby reminded her of. She snapped her fingers. "*The Clue in the Old Inn*!"

"The what?" Chef Antonia asked.

"Deena Morales Mystery #2! This place looks *exactly* like the inn from *The Clue in the Old Inn*!"

"You're right," Willow said, looking around. "I can't believe I never noticed that before!"

Evie looked meaningfully at Willow.

Willow looked meaningfully at Evie.

Pierce scowled. "What's happening?"

Willow turned to face the others. "*The Clue in the Old Inn* is a murder mystery," she explained.

"An old-fashioned whodunit," Evie added.

"A who-what-it?" Francesca asked.

"Who. Done. It," Willow spelled out. "Six strangers all check into an old inn on the same weekend. One of them is murdered, and the rest of them have to piece together the clues to figure out who did it. The whole thing ends with this awesome dinner party scene where teenage detective Deena Morales solves the mystery and the murderer is revealed!" She turned to Evie. "Could we do something like that?"

"Sure we could!" Evie could practically feel her brain whirring into action. "We could stage a fake murder, hide some clues, then do the dinner party. Maybe without the poisoned goblet, though," she amended.

"The *what*?" Pierce exclaimed.

"No, not the goblet," Willow agreed quickly. "We should totally do the séance, though!"

"Oh, definitely the séance!"

Pierce's eyes narrowed. "You're talking about books? The Deena . . . Munroe . . . Murphy . . ."

"Deena *Morales*," Willow corrected him.

"Whatever! You're saying we should base the most important night of our careers and the future of this entire hotel on a junk novel?"

Willow and Evie both gasped.

"They are *not* junk novels!" Evie insisted.

"They're bestsellers," added Willow. "And there's a reason for that—people love mysteries!"

"They have a point, Pierce," Bree said thoughtfully. "Actually, this might be exactly what we need to keep up social media interest! My 'Meet the Ghosts of the Ivan' series has been going pretty well. We've gained a bunch of new followers lately. But a murder mystery dinner party would be even better! Maybe we could livestream it?"

"And we could come up with *such* a wonderful menu!" Francesca enthused, shaking Antonia's arm.

Evie looked triumphantly at Willow. But instead of happy, Willow looked suddenly uncomfortable.

"It's a good idea," she said, wringing her hands. "But before we go any further, there's something I need to say."

Evie frowned—was Willow blinking back tears?

"We have to face the possibility that this might not work. Even if the inspector has a good time, he might not rank us number one. We might not get any more guests. After what happened to Anna, and to Leo and Alford . . . I know you're all starting to Fade."

There was a loud cacophony of denials, but Willow waved them off.

"You're all trying to hide it from me. But I'm not an idiot. You're all struggling. Even Cuddles is . . . well . . ." She gestured to the site of his latest accident. "There's enough money left in the Rainy Day Fund to keep things running until a few days after the inspector is here. But that's it. If the inspector doesn't give us a number-one ranking in *Zagged*, we'll have to fold."

Evie took a deep breath. She'd suspected that things were worse than Willow had let on, but she'd had no idea things were this dire. What had she gotten herself into?

Bree, Pierce, and Antonia all exchanged pointed glances.

"We've been talking about that," Bree said. "The Ivan's money situation, I mean."

"I don't have much to offer," Antonia cut in. "I'm still paying off Francesca's culinary school loans. But I have a little bit saved."

"And I've been saving to open my photography studio," added Bree. "But if you need the money—"

"I've got a bit put away in a bank account," Molly added. Then, after a pause, "I'm not entirely sure which bank. But I'm sure I could figure it—"

Pierce waved them all silent. "If the Ivan needs a loan, I'd be happy to oblige," he said. "I've got plenty of money."

"You *do*?" Evie exclaimed, unable to hide her shock. Even though most ghosts were paid fair wages, the government put such an enormous death tax on NCE earnings that most ghosts had trouble saving money. With the exception of Kathleen Deetz, the ghost billionaire, wealthy ghosts were almost unheard of.

"I've been working at the Ivan since 1619," Pierce informed her. "That's four hundred years of wages. I'm not a billionaire or anything—I've made a few bad investments here and there—but I have enough to help."

"That's very generous of you guys," Willow said. "But it

wouldn't be fair for the Ivan to take your money. And even if it was," she added hastily when Pierce opened his mouth to argue, "it's not really money we need right now. Mercer is a small town. There's not enough room, and not enough guests, for two haunted hotels. We need the *Zagged Guide* to rank us number one again so the guests will come back. If we can't do that, all the money in the world won't matter."

"And you really think this murder mystery idea will work?" Pierce asked.

"It's a good idea," Willow said hesitantly with a glance at Evie. "But I don't know if I can ask you all to risk your afterlives on it. None of you has to stay at the Ivan. I can go on GhouledIn right now and give you all the highest possible rankings, the most glowing and enthusiastic references. None of you would have any trouble finding other jobs. Maybe even at a Hauntery, where you'd never have to worry about Fading."

"But Willow, if the Rainy Day Fund is almost gone, what will you do if we all leave?" Molly asked. "And your mother! What would happen to your mother?"

"You can't think about that now," Willow said quickly. "You all have to think about yourselves."

There was a long silence. Evie held her breath as the staff of the Hotel Ivan looked around at one another. Nobody, it seemed, wanted to be the first to speak.

Finally, Bree cleared her throat. "When I died, it took me nearly twenty years to learn to manipulate objects on the mortal plane. Far longer than most. Willow's grandfather, Hector Ivan, kept me on anyway. An office manager who couldn't do a lick of work for *twenty years*. 'This is your home, Bree,' he said. And it's *still* my home. I want to open my own business one day—hopefully someday soon. But I'm not leaving while the Ivan is in trouble. I'm staying, Fading or no Fading."

The rest of the staff looked uncertain. Evie saw Willow look over at Pierce.

Pierce let out a tremendous sigh. "Back when I was Living—a long, long time ago, mind you—I was a sailor on a, er, Spanish trading vessel—"

"It was a pirate ship," Bree whispered to Evie, loud enough that the entire room could hear. "Pierce was a pirate."

"What?" Willow asked incredulously.

"I was a *merchant sailor*," he corrected, looking a shade more annoyed than usual. "But I didn't care for that life. So when we made landfall in Florida, I left the ship and headed north. I had no money, no prospects. No manners, really. But Gracey Ivan—your five-times-great-grandmother, Willow—had just built a hotel called the Ivan. She hired me to work in the kitchen. I wanted to repay her for her kindness. And I did, for decades. But then, one night, I left a lantern too near the woodpile . . ."

He trailed off.

"That's how that fire started?" Willow asked. "I never knew that!"

"It was me," Pierce said reluctantly. "I burned down the whole kitchen, half of the Ivan, and myself. Gracey knew. She forgave me. She never told anyone. She could have, and I never would have found another job. I almost certainly would have Faded within the year. Instead, she asked me to be the Ivan's first resident ghost."

Pierce swallowed. "I don't know about this plan. A whodunit? A séance?" He winced. "What I do know is that this hotel has been my entire death's work. I remember every moment I've spent here. I intend to have many more moments here before I Fade. I'm staying, too."

Willow nodded, and Evie was standing close enough to hear her let out a very long, relieved breath.

"I haven't been here as long as some of you," Chef Antonia said. "But I *have* finally managed to organize the pantry and the freezer exactly how I like them. Only an idiot would walk out on that much work."

Francesca laughed out loud at that. "I'm staying, too," she announced, linking arms with her aunt. "I still have a lot to learn."

Molly stood up. "I'm in as long as I get to play the murder victim!" she declared. "I may not remember how I died the first time, but at least now I can fake die for a good cause!"

"That makes sense," said Willow with a smile. She looked around the room with tears in her eyes. "I love you all so very much. Thank you."

Evie shook her head in disbelief.

"What?" Willow asked her.

"Nothing," Evie said. "This is just a very different kind of staff meeting than the ones at my other job."

"Welcome to the Ivan." Willow smiled. "Now, let's get to work."

CHAPTER 11
WILLOW

Willow stretched, adjusting her position on the over-stuffed red couch while being careful not to disturb the laptop balanced on her knees. Behind her, Evie was pacing the length of the lobby with one finger tapping her chin.

"Read me back what we have so far?" the Ivan's new Phantasm requested.

Willow frowned down at the laptop. "Lights up on a cozy hotel lobby," she read. "The hotel guests have assembled for a cocktail party. Hotel employees are arranged about the room. Vampire Concierge is behind the front desk. Murder Victim enters—"

"We can't keep calling our characters Vampire Concierge

and Murder Victim," Evie pointed out. "We're going to have to come up with actual names at some point."

"For the Vampire Concierge . . . I guess we can just call him Pierce," Willow suggested. "Since . . . well, since he *is* Pierce. In a vampire costume."

"*Count* Pierce," Evie suggested. "Vampires are counts, right? Like Count Dracula?"

"That'll work," Willow said, typing. "And 'Murder Victim' is Molly, but we can't just call her Molly. It should be something more mysterious. More ominous."

"And important sounding," Evie added. "Grand. Lofty."

Willow racked her brain for an appropriately eerie yet snooty-sounding name. It was hard to think when the hotel was so uncharacteristically quiet. They still didn't have a single guest. Which was actually just as well, since everyone at the Ivan was hard at work getting ready for the upcoming whodunit. Francesca and Antonia had their heads together in the kitchen, coming up with the dinner party menu. Bree had been on the phone all morning, trying to drum up some sympathetic local publicity. Pierce was spiffing up the dining room, and Molly was, as usual, searching for her head.

Willow had assigned herself and Evie the task of writing the scripts for the murder and séance scenes. She'd put the whole morning aside for the task, which had seemed like more than enough time at first. She and Evie had settled in beside a crackling fire, happily brainstorming murder mystery ideas with only the sound of Cuddles's cute little snores in the background.

But now the clock on the mantel was inching toward noon, and they still hadn't even finished the murder scene, let alone moved on to the séance. Cuddles's snores were getting less adorable and more obnoxious by the minute, and with only three days until the inspector was due to arrive, Willow was getting anxious that they wouldn't finish the script in time to rehearse properly.

"Writing is harder than I thought it would be," Willow confessed.

Evie nodded in agreement. "How does the Deena Morales author do it?"

"You mean Angelina Garcia?" Willow put the laptop aside, picked up *The Clue in the Old Inn*, and started thumbing through it. "I don't know! She comes up with dozens of character names for every book. Who knew it would be so hard?"

"Why don't we call the Murder Victim Mrs. Morales?" Evie suggested.

"Deena's last name?" Willow considered this. "It's not very ominous. And isn't using one of Angelina Garcia's names sort of . . . stealing?"

"We're not stealing, we're borrowing," Evie insisted. "It's an *homage*. We're paying tribute to the character who inspired us!"

"I guess we could do that," Willow agreed hesitantly. "Mrs. Morales . . . no, *Baroness* Morales!"

"Love it!" said Evie emphatically as Willow settled the laptop back onto her knees and started typing. "Whew! Moving on. How much more have we got to write?"

"The entire séance scene," Willow informed her.

Evie sank reluctantly down to the floor beside Cuddles. "I guess we need a cool name for the Medium, too, don't we?"

Willow opened her mouth to respond but closed it immediately as the sound of a wail and a large crash echoed from the dining room.

"What the—" Willow sprang up and headed toward the sound, Evie at her heels. They arrived in the doorway just as an even louder wail assailed their ears. It sent shivers down Willow's spine and brought with it a familiar sensation of heaviness.

Every piece of china the Ivan owned was laid out on the largest table in the center of the room. Pierce was standing in front of it, arms spread wide, placing himself between the valuable china and the white-nightgowned apparition in the corner.

"Eleanor," Pierce said calmly. "Your name is Eleanor Ivan. You're all right, Eleanor. Everything is—"

"*Where am I?*" Mrs. Ivan wailed, looking down at her feet. She was floating in the midst of an overturned tea trolley, her feet dragging through a pile of shattered teacups.

"You're in the hotel, Mom," Willow tried, going to stand beside Pierce. "In the dining room."

Mrs. Ivan frowned down at the ruined tea set. "I broke that," she announced, sounding like she was on the verge of wailing again.

"It doesn't matter," Willow said quickly. "It's not important."

"Eleanor, this is Willow," Pierce told her. "Your daughter. Remember?"

Mrs. Ivan drifted away from the overturned trolley, toward the door to the dining room. She stopped when she came face-to-face with Evie. "Willow . . ." she muttered. Her eyes widened. "What have you done to your hair?"

"Um." Evie raised a self-conscious hand to her locks, which were their natural flame red today. "Um, I don't think—"

"She's confused," Willow explained. "Mom, *I'm* Willow."

"Oh, Molly," Mrs. Ivan said with a distracted wave in Willow's direction. "I can't look for your head right now. I'm busy. Very busy . . ."

Evie leaped aside and allowed Mrs. Ivan to drift determinedly through the doorway.

Willow swallowed an enormous lump in her throat.

Pierce sagged with relief. "She came in out of nowhere," he explained, bending down to right the tea trolley. "Through the wall and into the tea set."

"She *touched* the tea set?!" Evie exclaimed, coming all the way into the room with a confused look on her face. "I thought she'd only been a ghost for a few months."

"Six months," Pierce corrected her, using a napkin to sweep the tea set shards into a pile. "WISPs can sometimes manipulate objects on the Living plane by accident. But they don't have any control."

"A WISP?" Evie asked. "You mean a Woefully Impermanent Spiritual—"

"She's not a WISP," Willow interrupted, not liking the shakiness in her voice. She knelt down beside Pierce and waved him away from the mess. "I've got this."

"I'll help you," Pierce insisted. "Let me—"

"I said I've *got it*!" Willow snapped.

Pierce stood up quickly, and Willow instantly regretted her words. She suddenly felt very alone on the floor. "I'm sorry," she said.

"It's all right," Pierce said, and Willow couldn't help but

notice he was using the same calming tone and the same words that he'd just used on her mother.

"Let's not tell my dad about this," Willow said, indicating the mess all around her. "He's already—I mean, I don't want him to worry."

Pierce set his napkin down on the table. "Willow, don't you think maybe he *should* be worried?"

"What?" Willow asked, confused.

Pierce knelt back down on the floor. "You shouldn't have to worry by yourself. He's your dad."

Willow shook her head. "He can't handle it right now."

"Why?" Evie asked. "What's wrong with your dad?"

"He suffers from depression," Pierce answered.

"He needs good news," Willow said. "I don't want to bother him until we have some."

And then, as though she'd heard Willow's words, Bree swept into the room. "The Channel 13 news crew is here!" she announced brightly, then drew back when she saw the mess on the floor. "What—"

"It's nothing," Willow said, standing up shakily. "Channel 13?"

"The same channel that runs Antonia's cooking show. They also do the *Mercer Evening News*," Bree clarified. "I told them all about our situation, and they're so into it— the beautiful, local, historic Ivan being threatened by the evil, soulless Hauntery that will stop at nothing to put us out of business! They want to do a story on us, and they're here to interview you. With cameras and everything."

"Cameras?!" Evie squealed, and Willow was puzzled to see her suddenly looking over her shoulder in terror. "Where?"

Bree jerked a thumb over her shoulder. "I've got them all set up outside by the stables. But they want to come in and get some footage of the inside, too."

"I've never done a TV interview before!" Willow said, nervously smoothing down the front of her shirt and wincing as a stray ceramic splinter dug into her thumb.

"It'll be great publicity," Bree assured her. "Everybody in Mercer watches Channel 13."

"I don't," said Pierce drolly. "I find them humorless and dull."

"*Everybody* watches it?" Evie asked, and Willow thought she looked oddly nervous again. Bree seemed to notice, too.

"Don't tell me you're camera shy, Ms. Phantasm," she teased Evie.

"No, no," Evie said, sounding flustered as she backed slowly out the door. "It's not that. It's just . . . I forgot I have an afternoon haunting scheduled. At the library. I don't want to be late."

"But the script!" Willow exclaimed. "We're not done!"

"Can we finish tomorrow?" Evie asked, taking another step back.

"I guess so, but—"

"Thanks!" Evie called, and if Willow hadn't known better, she would've said her new friend all but ran out the front door of the Ivan.

"What's with her?" Willow asked.

Pierce shrugged.

Bree rolled her eyes. "Phantasms," she said. "They're all such drama queens. Come on, let's get you ready to go on camera!"

CHAPTER 12
EVIE

From the moment she'd heard Bree utter the words *news crew*, all Evie could think about was how quickly those cameras could have busted the secret of her job at the Ivan wide open. She hadn't liked running out on Willow like that, not when they had so much to do. But she couldn't afford to take the chance of showing up on the evening news.

Back at the Hauntery, Evie did not have time to relax. She had six lengthy back-to-back hauntings with Louise, then, just as the sun was starting to go down, she found herself summoned to a mandatory emergency staff meeting. When she arrived at one of the Hauntery's state-of-the-art media rooms, she gulped as she spotted the *Mercer Evening News* logo splashed across the large projection screen.

Evie's nerves were humming as she, her parents (who had recently returned from their Phamazon job), and Louise gathered in a large clump with the rest of the Hauntery staff. Mr. Fox prowled around in front of the crowd. The colors of the projector image bounced off of his bald head as he walked. Once all of the Hauntery employees quieted down, he signaled to someone in the back of the room. The news logo faded, and Willow appeared on the screen, standing nervously beside a very blond reporter.

"And finally," the reporter said, "the story of a local landmark, the Hotel Ivan, which is fighting for its very existence now that the newest branch of the Hauntery has opened just a stone's throw away on Mercer Street. Here with us this evening is Willow Ivan, the daughter of the Hotel Ivan's owners. Willow, can you tell us what makes your hotel so special?"

"Um, yes," said Willow, who looked a bit startled as the reporter thrust a large microphone in front of her mouth. "My family has run the Hotel Ivan for the past four hundred years. We have twelve beautiful guest rooms, a restaurant with two Michelin stars and a celebrity chef, a rustic stable . . ."

As Willow continued to talk, lovely images of the Hotel Ivan floated across the screen—beautiful, whimsical snapshots (probably taken by Bree) that showed a warm, inviting, cozy haunted hotel.

Evie's mother sighed wistfully. "Such a charming place," she whispered to Evie too quietly for Mr. Fox to hear.

"It is," Evie agreed.

"Such a shame they'll be out of business soon," her mother finished, looking genuinely distressed for a moment before shrugging and turning her attention back to the screen.

"We're a family hotel," Willow went on, her voice getting slightly less shaky. "Most of our ghosts have been with us for several decades at least. As we say at the Ivan, *Haunt Local!*"

"Yet unlike the Hauntery, which boasts the slogan '*Hauntery ghosts never Fade*,' you are not able to make the same guarantee to your ghost employees, are you?" the newscaster said with a look of concern on her face that looked utterly fake to Evie. "We were all sad to hear about the recent Fading of your Terrifying Phantasm. Do you think your lack of a Phantasm is going to be the final nail in the Hotel Ivan's coffin?"

Evie bit her lip hard as Willow shook her head.

"We were all very sad to lose our dear Leo and his husband, Alford. But we have a very exciting and talented new Phantasm who will be debuting soon!"

Don't say my name, don't say my name, Evie begged Willow silently.

"We're all so thrilled to have her! She's just in time

to headline our new murder mystery whodunit!" Willow gushed, and as the camera panned away from her and back to the reporter, Evie wasn't sure whether she was about to explode with pride or sink to the floor with relief that her secret was still intact.

"We wish you the best of luck, Hotel Ivan," the newscaster said morosely, as though the Ivan had already died and they were all attending its funeral. "And now, on to your competition, the Mercer Street Hauntery."

A new bearded newscaster appeared onscreen, standing with Mr. Fox in front of the Hauntery.

"Thank you, Sheila! I'm here with Mr. Fox, the Hauntery's vice president of quality control. Mr. Fox, what do you say to accusations that your hotel conglomerate is heartlessly putting historic, family-run properties like the Hotel Ivan out of business?"

"We at the Hauntery Corporation pride ourselves on supporting the local communities we move into," Mr. Fox said into the microphone. "As you know, we are the world's biggest employer of NCEs . . ."

As Mr. Fox droned on, Evie's father leaned over to whisper to Evie's mother. "The Ivan has a new Phantasm?" he mused. "I wonder who they got?"

Me! Evie screamed internally. *Me, Dad! I'm the new Phantasm! The one they're so thrilled about!*

" . . . and we were so lucky to have the chance to restore

this gorgeous Mercer Street property to its former glory," Mr. Fox continued.

"Yes, about that," the newscaster broke in. "What do you say to those who claim that up until recently, the property we're currently standing on was nothing but an abandoned lot with an old gas station? What about the many longtime Mercer residents who say that this Victorian mansion didn't exist until the Hauntery built it late last year?"

Mr. Fox smiled wanly into the camera. "I'd say those longtime Mercer residents are *dangerously* misinformed."

"Well, there you have it!" the newscaster concluded. "The Hotel Ivan versus the Mercer Street Hauntery. Who will be number one? We'll find out when the *Zagged Guide* releases its new rankings next week. Back to you in the studio, Deborah!"

Mr. Fox pushed a button on the projector, and the video paused. He walked purposefully to the front of the room and faced the Hauntery staff.

"I've had just about enough talk of this *Hotel Ivan*," Mr. Fox said gloomily. "By next week, they will be just like every other tiny fleabag hotel the Hauntery has come up against—that is to say, the Hotel Ivan will *cease to exist*. In just a few days, the *Zagged* inspector will be with us, and I expect you all to give him the highest class of service you are capable of delivering. Are we clear?"

There were mumblings in the crowd.

"The news is right about this building being brand-new," a uniformed bellhop behind Evie whispered. "My buddy was part of the crew that built it. From scratch, he said. Nothing historical about it."

"What about the ghosts who haunt the Ivan?" a ghost standing somewhere to the right of Evie mused. "What will happen to them if the hotel goes under?"

"Who cares?" sneered Louise, fiddling with the sleeve of her suit jacket. "It's their fault for deciding to work at a substandard hotel in the first place."

"As you all know," Mr. Fox continued, drawing everyone's attention back to the front of the room, "I've been sent here by Corporate to *personally* oversee the launch of this property. No Hauntery Hotel has *ever* debuted as anything less than number one in its regional *Zagged Guide*. Should the *Zagged* inspector leave here with anything but the highest opinion of our hotel, I will find out why, and the employees who failed in their assignments will be terminated immediately."

There was a collective drawing of breath around the room.

"Impress the inspector," Mr. Fox ordered, "or take your chances with Fading. Remember, Hauntery ghosts never Fade. But each and every one of you can be replaced. Easily. Is that clear?"

There were mutterings and lots of nodding of heads.

"I *said*," thundered Mr. Fox, *"Are. We. Clear?"*

"Yes, Mr. Fox!" the staff chorused.

"Good. Dismissed!"

***

After the staff meeting, Evie's parents excused themselves to perform a scheduled haunting on the eighth floor.

"Don't we have a haunting later tonight, too?" Evie asked Louise.

"It was canceled," Louise informed her, then puffed up her chest. "Mr. Fox canceled it so that I can attend a meeting with him tonight. With people from *Corporate*. It's a teleconference that's bound to last for hours. He said it would be an excellent networking opportunity for me. It starts in just a few minutes."

"Have fun," Evie said dryly, though she couldn't imagine that anything occurring in the presence of Mr. Fox or Corporate could actually qualify as *fun*.

Louise raised an eyebrow. "I tried to tell you about the cancellation earlier today, but I couldn't find you."

"Oh?" Evie said, trying to look bored.

Louise narrowed her eyes. "Where were you?"

"Around," Evie said vaguely. "Why do you ask?"

"Because you're up to something," Louise said, looking Evie squarely in the face. "If you're thinking of trying to edge me out of this internship, think again. Mr. Fox is *delighted* with my performance so far. That's the word he used on my first evaluation form. *Delighted*."

"Believe me, Louise, I couldn't care less about your internship. It's literally the last thing in the world I'd want."

"Right," Louise said knowingly, clearly not believing a word Evie said. "I'm watching you, cousin. Whatever you're up to, I'm going to figure it out."

"Aren't you going to be late?"

Louise gave her one last smirk before leaving the room, and Evie shivered in spite of herself.

She'd hoped that Louise's internship would distract her from the fact that Evie had been spending so much time away from the Hauntery the past couple of days. Unfortunately, it seemed like Louise's new job responsibilities were making her more suspicious than ever. If Louise somehow found out about the Ivan, it would only be a matter of time before Mr. Fox knew. Then what? Would he really follow through on his threat to fire Evie and her parents?

Evie tried to force herself to calm down. Louise didn't know anything. She just had to be more careful, that was all.

And yet . . . knowing that both Louise and Mr. Fox were going to be in a meeting all evening was making her be the opposite of careful.

If Mr. Fox was lying about the Hauntery building being historic, what else was he lying about?

Reasoning that there was no way Deena Morales would

let an opportunity like this pass her by, Evie stole down the hallway toward Mr. Fox's office. The door was closed, and Evie would have bet money on the fact that it was locked. Apparently, Mr. Fox didn't have an overabundance of trust in the staff.

But of course, most of the staff, Evie included, were not terribly bothered by locks. Or doors.

Evie drifted through the door and stopped on the other side. The large desk in the center of the room was piled high with papers, but most of the office was empty. Mr. Fox was only at this Hauntery temporarily, and he hadn't brought many personal items with him. The bookshelf behind the desk contained only one framed photograph. It was of Mr. Fox standing with his arm around another tall, bald man who looked exactly like him. His brother, maybe? There was also an award for service to the Hauntery and a collection of books. Evie stepped around the desk to read some of the titles.

The Art of Effective Ghost Employee Management

Negotiation Tactics for Dealing with Non-Corporeal Employees

Dealing with the Dead: How to Get the Upper Hand in NCE Contract Negotiations

How to Gain the Respect of Your Ghost Employees in Twelve Easy Steps!

Evie doubted he'd gotten around to reading that last one.

She turned her attention back to the desk, where there was a laptop computer with a Hauntery screensaver, a pile of employee time sheets, and a stack of large leather journals. One of the journals was open to a spreadsheet with the title "Hotel Staff." Evie scooted around the desk to get a better look.

The spreadsheet had a column of names listed by hiring date. As the most recent Hauntery hires, she and her parents were at the bottom.

MacNeil, Evie. Spooky Little Girl. Difficult.

Evie grinned at this, then looked farther up the list until she came to:

Spengler, Patricia. Baker's apprentice (promoted to

assistant baker 2016). Faded.

Evie stared at the word, sure she'd read it wrong. But there it was in Mr. Fox's neat, precise handwriting: *Faded. Hauntery ghosts never Fade.*

Mr. Fox's well-worn copy of the *Official Hauntery Handbook* was lying next to the spreadsheet. It was shut. Evie flexed her fingers. She'd had large portions of the book read aloud to her, mostly by Mr. Fox when he was upset about something. But what if there was more in there?

Things Mr. Fox hadn't wanted to read out loud.

Evie flexed her fingers. She leaned down until her eyes were even with the book, put one finger against her thumb, and flicked.

The corner of the top cover jumped.

One more harder flick, and the cover opened entirely. The book fell open to a random page entitled "Acceptable Cobweb Draping Techniques."

Evie bit her lip. A book this boring would undoubtedly have an index. And if there was anything in this book about hotel staff Fading, it would be listed there.

Evie put her fingers in flicking position again, trying to flip as many pages of the book as she could at a time. It took her six attempts, and only two of her tries actually moved pages, but finally she was looking at the third page of the index.

E . . .

E . . .

F . . .

Fading, of Hotel Staff

A key jangled in the lock.

"I won't be a moment," came Mr. Fox's voice. "I forgot my—"

Evie ducked beneath the desk.

"—book," he finished.

There was a scraping sound on top of the desk, then a brief pause. A minute later, the door slammed shut again, and there was another jangle of keys. Evie waited under the desk for several moments anyway, too scared to move. When she was absolutely positive that Mr. Fox had left the office, she stood up and turned her attention back to the desk.

The *Handbook* was gone.

CHAPTER 13
WILLOW

N o no *no*!" came an outraged voice from inside the library.

There was a bark. Then Cuddles streaked into the lobby.

Willow leaned over the side of the scaffolding, trying not to drop the can of wallpaper paste in her hand. After she'd hired Evie, gotten an electrician to fix the fridge, and paid the linen service bill, there had been just enough money left in the Rainy Day Fund to buy new wallpaper for the lobby. But there hadn't been enough to pay a professional to put it up. Thank goodness for DIY videos on YouTube.

Willow watched as Cuddles paused to lift his leg against the wall in the corner, then shot off in the direction of the kitchen.

She frowned. Was she imagining things, or had Cuddles suddenly developed . . . fangs?

Pierce's angry voice rang out from the library again. *"I draw the line at Cuddles!"*

"But he looks so adorably menacing!" answered Evie's voice.

"He looks *ridiculous!*"

Willow climbed down from the scaffolding. In the library, she found Evie in full Phantasm costume squared off against Pierce . . . who was sporting a high-collared cape, a chalky-white complexion, and vampire fangs.

She and Evie had finished the script the day before yesterday, and since then, they'd had rehearsals almost nonstop. They'd had a fairly successful run-through that morning, but Evie had insisted on a final costume check that afternoon, just to make sure everybody would be picture-perfect for the inspector's arrival tomorrow. Willow had begged off in order to finish the wallpaper, but it seemed that no one else in the hotel had been spared from Evie's attentions, even Cuddles.

Molly stood beside Pierce. She was headless and dressed in a smart business suit, which Evie had deemed appropriate for a murder victim. Bree was in front of the mirror, wearing a long white wedding dress with a huge red stain on the chest. Francesca was wearing a mad scientist lab coat and adjusting the collar of Antonia's matching one.

Everyone seemed happy except Pierce, who looked to Willow like he was about to explode.

"Willow!" Evie clapped her hands together. "Good! What do you think of everyone's looks?"

"They're . . . um . . . I . . ." Willow stammered, desperately trying to avoid Pierce's glare.

"We've got to finish your detective outfit today as well," Evie said thoughtfully. Willow had been cast as Detective Ivan, who was heavily based on the character of Deena Morales. "Trickier, since you're not a ghost and you have to use real clothes. Your dad said he'd have a look in the attic and see what he could find for you."

"Dad said *what?*" Willow exclaimed. He'd been notably absent for several days now, and Willow had thought it best to leave him alone. "You've seen him today? He's *helping?*"

"You can see him yourself if you turn around," Evie said, and winked.

Willow spun on her heel and practically fell over as her father strode, very businesslike, into the room. He was wearing head-to-toe black with a police badge on one shoulder and a police cap on his head to match.

"Will this do for the Hapless Police Officer?" he asked. "I'm sorry I've missed so many rehearsals. But I memorized all of my lines."

Willow and Evie exchanged glances. They'd written

only two very short lines for the Hapless Police Officer, and they'd given Mr. Ivan the part because they'd pretty much assumed he wouldn't be participating.

"That's great, Dad," Willow said heartily as a warm feeling started to spread through her chest.

Mr. Ivan fiddled with his sewn-on police badge, suddenly looking a tad anxious.

"I—I was going to find some things for you, too, Willow. In some of your mother's old boxes. But . . . I . . . I couldn't—"

"That's all right," Willow put in quickly. "Don't worry about it, Dad. I'll find an outfit myself later." Then, because discussing her mother appeared to have deflated him, she added enthusiastically, "You're going to make a great police officer."

Mr. Ivan nodded, muttered something about practicing his lines, and shuffled out of the room.

Willow was practically floating as she exited the library and made her way back toward the scaffolding. Pierce trailed after her, still scowling.

"Pierce, did you see that? Dad was out of the office. Fully dressed!"

"Yes, I saw. But Wil—"

"He even memorized his lines! I wonder if—"

"*Willow!*"

Willow jumped, tore herself from her thoughts, and faced the concierge, who had already transformed his clothes back into his usual black suit and impeccably neat muted tie.

"Is it the outfit, Pierce? Because you don't have to be a vampire, you know. I'm sure Evie could—"

"I don't care what kind of outfit it is. I care that I'm being required to wear a costume *at all*. Never, in all of my years at the Ivan, have we entertained such ridiculousness."

"It's only for one night, Pierce. It won't kill you, it—"

Pierce raised his eyebrows, and Willow cut herself off.

"I'm sorry," Willow muttered. "That's not what I meant to say."

Pierce took a deep breath. "I know I promised I'd give all of this a chance. But vampires? Corpse brides? Mad scientists in the kitchen?"

"I don't know, I think the mad scientists are kind of cool—"

Pierce's scowl deepened, and Willow swallowed her attempt at levity. "Is it Evie?" she asked him. "You haven't been very nice to her, you know."

"She's no Leo."

"No, she's not Leo," Willow agreed. "She's not supposed to be Leo. She's supposed to be *Evie*. She's great."

"She's hiding something. There's something she's not telling us."

Willow rolled her eyes. "What could she possibly be hiding? She has good ideas. This whole whodunit thing is—"

"It's in poor taste," Pierce fumed. "It's undignified."

"Honestly, Pierce, you can be so old-fashioned sometimes."

"Good taste never goes out of fashion! And taste aside, this is not us. This is not how we do things at the Ivan! I don't see why we can't just be ourselves—"

"We can't be ourselves right now, Pierce."

"Why not?"

"Because we can't."

"But why—"

"Because being ourselves *isn't good enough*!" Willow exploded.

Pierce's eyes widened, and he took a small step backward.

Willow took a deep breath. "If being ourselves were enough," she said, trying to rein in her temper, "then Leo and Alford would still be here. We'd have a hotel full of guests. We wouldn't care about the stupid Hauntery, and my mother wouldn't be half-Faded and wandering around the hotel like a—" Willow broke off, shocked at herself.

"Like a *what*?" Pierce asked carefully.

"Nothing, I—"

"Like a *ghost*?"

"No!"

It sounded so shameful when Pierce said it like that. Shameful, and not even accurate. There was still some debate about whether her mother was a WISP or not—Willow still wasn't ready to admit that possibility to herself. But whether she was a WISP or not, her mother was definitely a ghost. Willow wasn't sure she had allowed that thought inside her head before.

"What I mean," she continued, "is that if we want to beat the Hauntery, we have to adapt. People want scary. So we're going to give them scary! Even my dad seems to understand how important this is, Pierce. Why can't you?"

"All right," Pierce said, throwing up his hands in surrender. "I'll wear the vampire outfit, if that's what you really—what? What are you staring at?"

Willow swallowed, suddenly at a loss for words. She was staring at Pierce's left hand.

Or, more specifically, at the area above the stump of his wrist, where his hand used to be.

"Oh." The concierge quickly tucked his arm behind his back.

"You—you're Fading?" Willow could barely breathe.

"It's not as bad as it looks," Pierce tried to assure her, but Willow felt like somebody had kicked her in the stomach.

"Why didn't you tell me?"

"I didn't want to worry you," Pierce said gruffly. "It's all right. Really."

"No," Willow said emphatically, blinking back tears. The strain of knowing that she couldn't throw her arms around Pierce's skinny waist and hug him as tightly as she could was almost unbearable. "It's not all right. It's not all right at all!"

"We still have time," Pierce reminded her gently. "I'm not Faded yet."

"I can't lose you," Willow said. "The Ivan wouldn't be the Ivan without you!"

Pierce smiled. Not his usual pinched, barely tolerant smile. A tiny, honest grin. It transformed his entire face while somehow also being the most Pierce-like expression Willow had ever seen. "Then we'd better get to work," he said, clearing his throat. "For the Ivan."

"For the Ivan," Willow echoed. Then, after a moment, "I'll ask Evie to get rid of Cuddles's fangs."

"Thank you," Pierce said quietly.

CHAPTER 14
EVIE

Before Willow and Pierce's argument, Antonia and Francesca had managed to slip out of the library and make themselves scarce. But when the argument really started to heat up, Evie, Molly, and Bree had found themselves trapped. Not wanting to eavesdrop but unable to keep from overhearing the entire exchange, they stood quietly behind the library doors until the silence on the other side told them that both Willow and Pierce had left the lobby.

Evie looked warily at Molly and Bree, wondering if they'd caught Pierce's accusation of her.

She's hiding something . . .

To Evie, it was as though Pierce had said those words over a loudspeaker. But neither of the others seemed to have heard them the same way. Bree sat down with her back to the still-closed door and pulled out her phone. Molly wandered over to the big mirror. She kept changing her clothes back and forth from her murder victim outfit to her Medium robes—she was playing both roles. She was headless, so Evie wasn't sure why exactly she needed to be in front of a mirror, but at least she was occupied.

Evie lingered near the door.

"Um, Bree?"

"Hmm?"

"You said something before about how it took longer than usual for you to touch objects on the Living plane?"

Bree looked up from her phone. She'd been scrolling through her Instagram feed. "Yeah. It took me twenty years."

"Do you know why it took so long?"

"I have an idea, yes. And I'm glad it did."

"You're—you're *glad*?" Evie sputtered, certain she couldn't have heard Bree correctly.

"Sure." Bree put her phone down and shifted so she was sitting cross-legged. At some point during the argument, she'd exchanged her corpse bride outfit for normal clothes: skinny jeans and a T-shirt that read WALLS TURNED SIDE-WAYS ARE BRIDGES. —ANGELA DAVIS. From the little Evie had learned about Pierce, she was pretty sure he'd have a fit if he saw Bree (or any employee) wearing denim in the workplace. Then again, since there were no guests in the hotel, the whole staff had been pretty casual lately. Evie was still wearing her Phantasm cloak over a black leotard and leggings, but part of her was itching to change into jeans herself.

"I had a hard time coming to terms with my death," Bree explained. "I had a lot of plans for my life, you know? I was a bit in denial about being a ghost, which made it difficult to master ghost skills. During those years when I couldn't touch anything, all I could do was observe. I got *really* good at it. It got to where I would notice things that not everyone else did. That was how I developed my photographer's eye. I'm not sure that would have happened if I'd been able to touch objects right away."

"Oh," Evie said. She slumped down to sit on the floor beside Bree, her Phantasm cloak settling around her like a blanket.

"What's wrong? Are you having a little trouble in that area?"

"I've been practicing," Evie said quickly, lest the Ivan's office manager think she was just lazy and whining. "On books, and pencils, and anything else I can find. Sometimes it works. Other times, I think I'm getting close, but then my fingers just go right through it!"

Bree nodded and picked up her Nikon. She handled it

delicately. Her fingers, nails bright with sparkly silver polish, played over every inch of its matte black surface.

"My cousin thinks I'm stupid to even try to pick things up so soon," Evie confessed. "My parents, too." *And Mr. Fox*, she added silently.

"Practice helps," Bree offered. "The very first thing that I touched was a camera. Not this one." She held up the Nikon. "An older model. Willow's grandmother, Winifred Ivan, bought it for me. The second I saw it—I'd never wanted to hold something so badly in my life. Or in my death. To touch it. To use it. To express the way I'd learned to look at the world."

"I see," Evie said, rather disappointed. She hated to admit it, but she'd been hoping for a shortcut. Twenty years seemed like such an interminably long time, and she didn't have anything like Bree's camera to motivate her. "So, there's no shortcut? No trick?"

"Sorry," Bree said with a smile. "I can only tell you what worked for me. And that was wanting it badly enough. But you? It seems like with you, it's more a crisis of confidence. You don't *believe* you can do it. And no wonder, with all that negativity around you."

"They're my family," Evie said reluctantly.

"Family or not, there are always going to be people who underestimate you," Bree said. "Sometimes, it can be tempting to believe what others think about you—it's easier, in a weird way. But if you want to do great things, you've got to believe you can. Nobody's going to believe it *for* you. They can't—not in the same way. Make sense?"

"Yeah," Evie said, thinking hard. "I think it does—"

Click.

Evie jumped.

"Smile," Bree commanded from behind the lens of the Nikon. "I don't have a portrait of you yet."

"A portrait? For what?" Evie asked, awkwardly trying to speak and hold a smile at the same time.

"For the 'Meet the Ghosts of the Ivan' series on Instagram," Bree answered.

"Instagram?" Evie fought down a wave of panic. "I don't know—I mean, I don't—"

"You don't like to be on social media?" Bree guessed. "No worries. I respect that. But let me get a picture anyway, just for us here in the hotel? After all, you *are* a ghost of the Ivan now, aren't you?"

After a moment's hesitation, Evie smiled. Bree raised the camera again.

"Hello?" interrupted an authoritative voice from the lobby.

Bree and Evie pulled each other to their feet and reached the lobby at the same time as Molly. There was a police officer there, looking around uncertainly at the scaffolding.

"Can we help you?" Molly asked.

"Yes, I—oh!"

Evie bit back a giggle as the officer jumped at the sight of the Headless Horsewoman.

"Oh *my*," the officer exclaimed. As he straightened his hat and endeavored to compose himself, his stunned expression faded to one of awe. He took a step closer to Molly, looking her up and down with avid curiosity. Evie stiffened, quite sure that Molly would be offended by such rudeness if she had eyes at the moment to see what was happening.

"Well, you're *marvelous*, aren't you?" the officer muttered.

"Yes," Molly replied. "I am."

"Did you need something?" Evie asked, her voice coming out every bit as sharply as she intended it to. The officer's attention shifted toward her, and he regained his former gruff expression. He fished a grainy photo out of his pocket, squinted at it, then squinted back at Evie.

"You're not Willow Ivan, are you?" he asked uncertainly, looking down at the photo again. From her angle, Evie could just barely make out a blurry, black-and-white image of Willow and her father. The photo looked like it might be an old newspaper clipping.

"No," Evie answered the officer. "I'm not Willow. My name is Evie MacNeil."

"Do you have any identification to that effect?" the officer asked as Bree stepped up to stand beside Evie.

"I'm a non-corporeal entity," Evie replied matter-of-factly. "So, no."

"Oh, right, of course!" The officer's eyes flashed between Evie and Bree, then back over to Molly.

"Is—" He broke off and looked around, lowering his voice to a conspiratorial whisper. "Is this a *haunted* hotel?"

A tiny, mean-spirited part of Evie wanted to say no to see how the officer would react. Instead, she lowered her voice to match his and said, "Yes."

The officer's eyes widened as he put the photo back into his pocket. "I've always wanted to stay in a haunted hotel!" he admitted with such enthusiasm that Evie half expected him to clap his hands and jump up and down like an excited five-year-old. "I'm thinking of booking a weekend at that new place everybody's talking about. What's it called? The Haun—"

"We're very busy here, Officer," Bree interrupted him. "Did you say you were looking for someone?"

"Yes," the officer said, attempting to regain an air of seriousness and importance, even as he kept stealing excited glances around the lobby. "Might I speak to Miss Ivan?"

"She's not here," Evie said quickly. "I'm not sure when she'll be back."

"How about her father, Mr. Ivan?"

Evie hesitated. She couldn't quite put her finger on why, but her gut was telling her very strongly that she needed to keep this police officer far away from Mr. Ivan and Willow. When she looked over at Bree hesitantly, she could tell that the Ivan's savvy office manager was thinking the same thing.

"He's gone for the day as well," Bree lied swiftly. "Might we give them a message?"

The police officer looked disappointed. He dug into another one of his pockets, pulled out a business card, and held it out to Evie, who was standing closest to him. Evie stepped forward automatically to take it. Her fingers were inches away when she stopped, flushed with embarrassment, and stepped back.

"Come on, then," the officer said impatiently, waving the card in the air.

Evie, liking this police officer less and less with each passing moment, glared at him. "I am only recently non-corporeal, sir," she informed him. "I can't—"

"Oh." The officer looked embarrassed. "My apologies, miss, I meant no offense. I've received *thorough* training on the subject of non-corporeal entities—NCEs—of course. But I haven't come across many in my current assignment."

"What assignment is that?" Bree asked.

"Department of Truancy."

"Ah!" Molly snapped her fingers. "You mean you're the one who makes sure that kids aren't skipping school?"

"Exactly, ma'am," said the officer, and Evie was suddenly incredibly glad she'd lied about Willow's and her dad's whereabouts.

"I've been applying for a transfer to NCE Relations for years," the officer said as Bree stepped forward to take the business card out of his hand. "But so far, no luck. It's all about who you know, isn't it?"

"I guess so," Evie said, eager to be rid of the officer before one of them accidentally blew their lie. "Don't worry, we'll see that Ms. Ivan gets your card, Officer . . . ?"

"Myers. Officer Harry Myers. Please tell Ms. Ivan and her father to contact me immediately. Truancy is a very serious matter." He tipped his hat to them. "Good day to you all."

When he was gone, Bree let out a loud sigh. "*The Living,*" she scoffed. "Always in such a hurry. Always thinking they're *so important.*"

"That's what *I'm* always saying!" Evie exclaimed.

Bree leaned over to toss the officer's card into the bin beside the front desk, and Evie felt marginally better. If Bree wasn't worried, maybe there really was nothing to worry about.

Back in the library, Molly did another spin in front of

the mirror. "I don't think this Medium costume is right. I can't see what it looks like, but it *feels* off. What do you think?"

"Maybe we could go in a different direction," Bree said. She stood up, glancing at her phone. "It's three o'clock right now. We still have twenty-four hours to get it right before the inspector gets here."

"Three?" Evie exclaimed. She hadn't realized it had gotten so late. "I'd better go. I've got a . . . a . . ."

"Library haunting?" Bree guessed.

"Um, yeah," Evie mumbled, realizing that lying about her job at the Hauntery was getting harder every time she had to do it. Especially when Bree smiled at her the way Evie imagined an older sister would.

"See you tomorrow, Ms. Phantasm."

Evie ran full speed through the back door of the Hauntery.

"You're *late*," snapped Louise.

"Sorry," Evie said, not feeling sorry at all. "I got held up."

"You're not even changed!"

Evie sighed heavily, closed her eyes, and willed the hideous pink dress to appear. Before she could even look down to see if she'd gotten it right, Louise grabbed her hand and dragged Evie toward the lobby.

"The inspector is here, getting checked in," she announced over one shoulder. "We're supposed to do our act for him. Then he's going to a private cocktail party with Mr. Fox and some people from Corporate, which your mother will haunt. Then there's dinner, and your father's Phantasm performance during dessert. But we're his first impression, so we need to be perfect. Oh, Evie. Ugh!"

She stopped and dropped Evie's hand, glaring disapprovingly.

"What?" Evie demanded, looking down at her outfit. It was just as pink and ruffly as usual.

"Your *hair*," Louise said accusingly. Then she closed her eyes, and Evie felt the hair on either side of her head spring up into two very tight, bouncy pigtails.

"I can do that myself, you know," Evie growled. "I hate it when you—"

"We have to be *perfect*!" Louise huffed, and began hauling Evie toward the lobby again. "Mr. Fox has made me the inspector's official ghost liaison. As soon as our act is over, I get to escort him around for the rest of the evening!"

"Congratulations," Evie muttered as they approached Mr. Fox, who was standing beside another man at the front desk.

"Ah, girls, there you are," Mr. Fox said with a huge, forced smile, but also a glint in his eye that told Evie they were late. He gestured to the man beside him. "This is Mr. Renard, the most senior inspector on staff at the *Zagged Guide*. Mr. Renard, these are the Hauntery's Spooky Little Girls."

"Splendid!" Mr. Renard effused. He was tall, the same height as Mr. Fox. But unlike Mr. Fox, Mr. Renard had a huge mop of thick blond curls atop his head. Beneath all of his hair, the hotel inspector had beady little eyes that reminded Evie of something . . . maybe a squirrel. They seemed to look at everything at once, not missing a single detail. "What a wonderful way to start."

"Welcome to the Hauntery, Mr. Renard," Louise said grandly, then stretched her fingers out toward Evie.

With a sigh, Evie took Louise's outstretched hand and forced her voice into the familiar monotone.

"Play with us!" they chorused. "Play with us . . . forever!"

CHAPTER 15
WILLOW

Willow couldn't sleep, so she wandered.

By this time tomorrow evening, the whodunit would be over. The inspector would either be impressed or not, and it would be too late to do anything else to change his mind. The fate of the Ivan would be decided, one way or another.

Sleep, under these circumstances, was impossible.

So Willow wandered.

She walked through the kitchen—spotless, in preparation for tomorrow—meandered through the lobby—which was looking a shade nicer than usual, even if it still smelled faintly of wallpaper paste—and finally drifted down the first-floor hallway, where she winced under the gaze of all the portraits. All those former Ivans. All of them had probably done a better job of running the hotel than Willow had.

I don't want to be the Ivan who loses the hotel!

She found her mother in the music room.

Mrs. Ivan was floating in front of the piano, her nightgown swirling behind her as she trailed one hand delicately and soundlessly over the tops of the keys.

Willow closed her eyes and remembered the way her mother used to play the piano, the way she used to be able to tap out an entire song after hearing it once. Willow had never had her mother's talent, but that hadn't stopped her from practicing. She'd spent hours in this very room, sitting before this very instrument. But that had been before. Ever since that fateful Friday, Willow had hardly been able to look at the piano without tearing up.

Willow opened her eyes. Her mother was staring right at her.

"Hi," Willow said.

The ghost blinked but said nothing. Willow wasn't sure if she'd really been seen. She waited, bracing herself against the suffocating, choking feeling of loss that always seemed to follow her mother's ghost around.

But it didn't come. There was no blanket of grief settling around her head, no crushing, drowning feeling in her chest. The air didn't thicken, she was able to breathe normally, and she felt no inexplicable urge to start sobbing. Instead, Willow found that she felt rather numb. Like she had no feelings inside of her at all, good or bad.

That should have been better, shouldn't it? Better than soul-crushing grief, the feeling of drowning on dry land? Willow had been waiting for her bad feelings to ebb, hoping they would disappear one day. But now that they had, she felt . . . worse. Much worse.

Numbness was worse than drowning.

Willow sighed and sat down onto the piano bench. "It's a big day tomorrow," she said. Mrs. Ivan stopped over by the left side of the instrument, her gaze locked dreamily on the side of Willow's face. "We're ready, I think. We've rehearsed a lot. Pierce still hates the vampire outfit, but . . . well, you know Pierce."

A tiny smile appeared on the ghost's lips at that.

"We're ready," Willow said again. "We're either going to knock the socks off that inspector and get back to number one, or . . ."

Willow trailed off. Her mother looked away, then drifted around to the far side of the piano.

"Or we'll have to close," Willow muttered, hovering her fingers over the keys, her thumbs above middle C. "Hopefully, the ghosts will find new places to go. But I'm afraid they've waited too long, taken too much of a chance by staying here."

Willow pressed her fingers down to try a tentative chord. The notes sounded jarring. Off-key. *Wrong.*

Willow took her hands off the keys.

"Pierce has already started to Fade," she said quietly. "Antonia, too. And Cuddles. And you—"

The ghost paused to stare at the heavy drapes that covered the windows.

"Actually, I don't know what will happen to you," Willow mused. "No matter what the inspector says tomorrow, I don't know how to help you, Mom. Any suggestions?"

The ghost turned and drifted through the bookshelf on the far wall, out of sight.

"I didn't think so," Willow said, slumping down on the piano bench, feeling like a balloon that had lost its air.

"You didn't think *what?*"

Willow's head snapped back up. Evie was in the doorway.

"I—um," Willow stammered. "I didn't think you'd be back until tomorrow morning."

"I wanted to do one more check," Evie admitted, coming farther into the room. "Plus, Molly's still looking for her head. I told her I'd help."

"I should help look, too," Willow said, but she made no move to get up from the bench.

Evie nodded to the piano. "Were you playing something?"

"No. It's out of tune."

"Oh." Evie took a breath. "I meant to tell you . . . a truancy officer came to the hotel today."

Willow felt herself grimace.

"He said he's been trying to get in touch with you. You or your father—"

"I'm handling it."

"Are you?"

"*Yes,*" Willow said curtly. With everything else that was at stake, Evie wanted to talk about *school*?

"*OK,*" Evie said with equal curtness.

They sat in silence for a long moment. Well, Willow sat. Evie stood awkwardly in the middle of the room, looking like she had forgotten what to do with her hands. She seemed nervous, and Willow wondered if it was just about the inspector coming tomorrow or something more. She was about to ask her what was wrong when Evie spoke instead.

"Did you make up with Pierce?" she asked.

"What?"

"I heard you guys yelling at each other."

"Oh," Willow said. "Yes, I apologized. He forgave me."

"Yeah?"

"Yeah. He knows I only mean, like, ten percent of the things I say when I'm mad. He's known me a long time."

"It must be nice to have people who understand you so well," Evie remarked.

Willow looked up. Evie had said those words in the same way she said most things. Boldly. Quickly. But there was something about the way she lingered over the word *people* and *understand* that made Willow suspect they meant something more to Evie.

"Your family . . ." Willow ventured. "They don't get the Phantasm thing, huh?"

"Nope, not at all," Evie confirmed.

"Is that why you took the job here? To prove something to them?"

"Sort of," Evie said, picking at some nonexistent lint on her black jeans. Her hair was in pigtails, Willow noticed. Cute, curly pigtails. Which didn't seem very Evie-like at all. "They think they know me. They think they know what I can do. But I've always hoped that they're wrong."

"I *know* that they're wrong. I saw you scare that kid at the library. You were wonderful."

"Yeah, but I've never actually done a full Phantasm act in front of a room full of people before," Evie admitted, absently twirling one of the pigtails around her finger. After a moment, she seemed to realize what she was doing and closed her eyes. Her hair transformed from the pigtails into a long, smooth, purple ponytail. "Tomorrow at the dinner will be my first time. My first real Phantasm cry."

"Is it ready?" Willow asked, trying not to sound concerned.

"I think it is," Evie said, and Willow thought she was trying to sound confident. "I've been practicing every spare moment I get."

"Then I know you'll be great," Willow said quite sincerely. "You know, Evie, I've been meaning to thank you."

"Me?"

"Yeah. With everything going on here, I didn't know what to do. Especially after Leo and Alford—" Willow paused, her throat suddenly dry. "I almost gave up. I was *ready* to give up. But you told me not to. You were the only one who told me not to!"

"Deena Morales wouldn't give up," Evie pointed out again. "Besides, I should be thanking *you*. Being a Phantasm is my dream—and you made it happen for me!"

"Well, I owed you one," said Willow.

"Friends don't keep score," Evie said seriously.

"Fair enough," Willow agreed with a smile. "No score."

Then, on a sudden hunch, Willow got up and walked

to the other side of the piano, near where her mother had disappeared.

"Willow?" Evie said quietly. "There's something I need to—"

"Hey, look!" Willow pointed down toward her feet. "Molly's head! I found it!"

Evie hurried around the piano. There was a severed head covered in brown curls at Willow's feet. Evie picked it up.

"Great," Evie said, and it seemed to Willow that her voice had suddenly gone choky.

"Sorry, what were you going to say?"

"Nothing," Evie said quietly, cradling Molly's head. "I wasn't going to say anything. Just . . . I think we're going to do an amazing job for the inspector tomorrow. I can feel it."

"Me too," Willow said.

"Me three!" Molly's head chimed in. "It's about time you found me. I've been down there for days! Cuddles must have had an accident somewhere nearby, because it smells *dreadful*!"

CHAPTER 16
EVIE

Mr. Renard, the hotel inspector, arrived at the Hotel Ivan at three p.m. sharp the next day.

Evie fingered her hair. She'd made it long, dark, and straight today, not wanting to take the slightest chance that Mr. Renard would recognize her as one of the Spooky Little Girls he'd seen perform at the Hauntery just yesterday.

Louise had been all smiles when the inspector checked out of the Hauntery that morning, so Evie could only assume that the rest of his stay had gone as well as the beginning.

But Evie tried to put that, along with the very existence of the Hauntery, out of her mind. It was the Ivan's turn to impress Mr. Renard. And so far, everything was going according to plan.

After he'd checked in and been shown his room, Mr.

Renard had been invited back down to enjoy a cocktail reception in the lobby with the other guests—and from the smile on his face, it seemed to Evie that he was really enjoying it. And so were the other guests.

Not that they were *real* guests, of course. The Ivan hadn't had any of those in weeks. It had been Bree's idea to comb through the Ivan's *Zagged* user ratings, find the raviest of rave reviews, and invite those guests back for a free weekend that would coincide with Mr. Renard's visit. Between Bree's efforts and the local news coverage they'd received, two parties had accepted their invitation: the Prescott family (composed of Mr. Prescott, Mrs. Prescott, and their thirteen-year-old daughter, Kylie) and Ms. Loustrous, an elderly woman who had brought her identical twin sister, also called Ms. Loustrous, with her.

Evie watched through a crack in the door of the STAFF ONLY room as Mr. Renard examined the painting above the fireplace. His mop of blond curls looked even fuller than it had the day before, as though he'd puffed it up. He had a Ms. Loustrous on either side of him, and he was smiling politely at each of them in turn. On the other side of the room, Mr. and Mrs. Prescott were helping themselves to apple cider and scones from the buffet. Kylie Prescott was stretched out in an armchair, looking at her phone.

Cuddles was curled up at Kylie's feet. Willow and Pierce were behind the front desk, and Bree was loitering inconspicuously on the other side of the lobby, dressed as a corpse bride, phone at the ready to livestream the scene to the Hotel Ivan's YouTube channel.

Molly and Mr. Ivan, also both in costume, were in position outside the front door, awaiting their cues (hopefully).

"OK, everyone," Evie whispered, mostly to herself, since everyone except for Pierce and Willow was too far away to hear her. "Exactly like we practiced."

She nodded to Bree, who nonchalantly reached her hand through the front wall of the hotel to signal Molly.

A moment later, Molly, head attached, clad in her neatly pressed murder victim business suit, strode into the hotel lobby.

"Your line, Willow!" Evie reminded her. "Remember to *enunciate.*"

"Why, hello, Baroness Morales," Willow said loudly and only a bit stiffly. "Welcome back to the Hotel Ivan."

"Thank you!" said Molly equally loudly as she leaned against the front desk, facing the rest of the lobby. The Ms. Loustrouses nudged Mr. Renard. Mr. and Mrs. Prescott both gestured to Kylie to put her phone away. Everyone seemed to sense that something was about to happen. Even

Evie, who had presided over the rehearsal of this scene at least fifty times, felt a tingle of excitement.

Molly took off her coat and swung it over one shoulder. "I'm thrilled to be here. Is my room ready?"

There was a pause.

"Pierce!" Evie whispered through clenched teeth. "So help me, if you don't—"

"But of course your room is ready," Pierce drawled in a reluctant but pitch-perfect Transylvanian accent. "We've been *dying* to have you back, Baroness."

Molly chuckled grandly, and Evie thanked her lucky stars that she hadn't had to come up with a real threat.

"Thank you, my dear Count Pierce," Molly said. "I'm looking forward to—what in the *world* is that?"

Willow signaled Bree, who turned off the lights. All of the drapes had been drawn before the party, so the room plunged into darkness, and Evie let out a loud scream. Not exactly a Phantasm cry—that would come later. This was just enough to give the room a taste of something scary.

A crash of thunder ripped through the three ancient speakers Pierce had resurrected from the attic and mounted in different parts of the lobby. Evie yelled again.

The lights flickered back on.

Molly was now lying facedown on the floor, her severed head several feet from her body.

The Hotel Ivan's murder mystery whodunit had begun.

"She's been murdered!" Bree shrieked, still filming the scene. "Baroness Morales has been *beheaded*!"

The Ms. Loustrouses tittered with glee and dragged Mr. Renard closer to the scene. The Prescotts closed in as well, until Molly's body was ringed with spectators.

"Someone call the police!" Willow screamed, and Evie looked expectantly toward the front door, hoping that Mr. Ivan remembered his cue.

But the man who walked through the front door of the hotel wasn't Mr. Ivan in his makeshift police uniform. It was a taller man clad in a *real* policeman's uniform, carrying an open notebook.

"Uh-oh," Evie muttered as Officer Myers walked to the middle of the lobby.

"The police?" he asked. "Who called for the police?"

Willow took a step around the desk, presumably to go deal with Officer Myers.

"No!" Evie whispered loudly, causing Willow to stop in her tracks. "You've got to hide. I'll deal with him."

"What?" Willow asked, looking confused.

"That's the truancy officer!" Evie hissed. "He's got a photo of you. Hide!"

Willow immediately ducked down behind the front desk. Evie wondered briefly how the officer had missed seeing Mr. Ivan, who was supposed to have been waiting just outside the hotel for his cue. But she didn't have time to dwell on that just now.

"Oh! A fake police officer!" one of the Ms. Loustrouses cried. "How fun!"

"I am a *real* police officer, madam," Officer Myers corrected her. "Officer Harry Myers, Department of Truancy. I'm looking for—"

"Officer Myers!" Evie enthused, running through the front desk to intercept him before he could speak to any more guests. "Welcome back! Your timing is perfect!"

"Oh?" The officer raised an eyebrow. "Has Ms. Ivan or her father returned?"

"Er, no. But they'll be back tomorrow morning," Evie lied, motioning Officer Myers toward the far corner of the lobby, out of earshot of the other guests. "I promise they'll give you a call then. Now, if you wouldn't mind—"

"I do mind, actually." Officer Myers stood his ground and pulled out a yellow piece of paper. "This here is a warrant to search the Hotel Ivan for any evidence of Mr. Ivan and/or Ms. Willow Ivan."

"A warrant?" Evie gulped.

"Yes," Officer Myers sniffed. "I won't be leaving here without answers."

"Of-of course not," Evie stammered, thinking fast. "It's—well, I was sure they'd gotten in touch with you about the private, VIP-only event? I know they meant to."

"I—VIP? Um, no, they didn't." Office Myers peered over Evie's shoulder at Molly's prone body. "That woman there. Is she—"

"She's fine," Evie said quickly. "That's Molly. You met her yesterday, remember?"

"But she's—"

"She's acting. You see, we're having a murder mystery here at the hotel tonight. And we're in need of a police officer."

Unfortunately, Mr. Ivan chose that very moment to appear in the Hotel Ivan's doorway. Luckily, Officer Myers had his back to the door and didn't see him, nor did he appear to notice Evie's pleading glance toward Bree.

"A police officer?" Officer Myers asked, stroking his moustache.

"Ours cancelled at the last minute," Evie told him as Bree frantically rushed Mr. Ivan back outside. "If you could possibly fill in, I'm sure Mr. Ivan and his daughter would be so grateful—"

"Ms. . . ."

"Evie."

"Ms. Evie." Officer Myers cleared his throat importantly. "As I've already told you, I have a warrant here to search the premises of the Hotel Ivan, and I can't leave until—"

"Oh, of course not! I'm not suggesting that you *leave*, Officer Myers!" Evie forced herself to laugh. "I'm suggesting that you *stay*. And search! And while you're searching, you can also lead the others in looking for clues to our whodunit!"

"Ms. Evie, this is an official police investigation, and I . . . I . . . Did you say 'whodunit'?"

"Yes! A *haunted* whodunit."

Officer Myers's eyes grew wide. "I've always wanted to do one of those," he whispered.

"I remember," Evie said.

"I wonder if the Hauntery offers anything like—"

"Oh, this one is *much* better," Evie assured him. "Please say you'll help us out? Mr. Ivan and his daughter will be back in the morning to clear everything up. And they'd be so happy to have you as their guest tonight. Dinner is included, of course."

"Dinner, you say?"

"Yes. We do *so* need an expert on non-corporeal entities,"

Evie added, doing her best to lay it on thick. "You'd be perfect for the job. Please say you'll stay?"

Officer Myers looked around, then glanced uncertainly at the warrant in his hand.

"I'll be able to talk to Mr. Ivan and his daughter in the morning?"

"Definitely."

"Well . . ." He looked down at the warrant one last time, then folded it in half and tucked it back into his pocket. "Well, why not? Why not indeed?"

He winked at Evie and strode toward the crime scene. "*Detective* Myers, at your service, folks! Give me some room, please. Beheading is a nasty business, and if we're going to get to the bottom of this, we're going to need to thoroughly examine the evidence."

Evie thought she might pass out with relief as she backed up to give the guests some room.

"Are you *crazy*?" Willow whispered at her from behind the front desk. "*I'm* supposed to play the detective!"

"Well, you can't do that now," Evie pointed out. "If he sees you, it's all over. He's going to have to be the detective. And the police officer."

"Why did you ask him to stay?"

"I was improvising!" Evie shot back. "He said he wasn't

going to leave! Would you rather I let him arrest you and your father in front of the inspector?"

"I guess not," Willow said reluctantly. "But what are we going to do about the rest of the evening?"

Evie took a deep breath. "I don't know. Things just got complicated."

CHAPTER 17
WILLOW

P ierce! Psssssst, Pierce. PIERCE!"

Pierce, jumping slightly at the summons, motioned Willow back inside the office and poked his head through the STAFF ONLY door.

"What's happening?" Willow demanded. "I need an update!"

As soon as Officer Myers, the inspector, and the rest of the guests had left the lobby to search the hotel for clues, Evie had waved Willow out from behind the desk and into the office. Willow had assumed it was a temporary move to keep her out of sight until they could come up with a new plan.

But as the minutes passed and nobody arrived to tell her the coast was clear, Willow had started to feel like the walls of the tiny, windowless room were closing in on her. After what felt like days had passed, and after deciding that there was no way she was spending her hotel's darkest hour trapped in an office, she had cracked open the door.

That was when she'd spotted Pierce.

"They're all upstairs," Pierce answered her. "They're searching the guest rooms for the murder weapon."

"OK, then, maybe I can sneak out of here and—"

"Better not," Pierce argued. "If Officer Myers sees you—"

"He won't!"

But Pierce remained where he was, blocking the doorway.

"Don't you think the police hauling away our hotel's owner and his daughter might negatively affect the inspector's report?"

Willow sighed. "Where's Dad?"

"With the others. We're passing him off as another hotel guest. He's wearing a beard so Officer Myers won't recognize him. He's doing fine."

"Well, if he can be out and about, I don't see why I—"

"We can't exactly put a beard on you, can we?"

"Pierce!" Willow whined desperately. "I can't sit here and do nothing!"

"You can," he said firmly, and Willow was annoyed to hear

that he was using his best concierge-dealing-with-a-difficult-guest voice. "If you want to help us now, that's exactly what you'll do, Willow. We've got this. OK?"

"Fine," Willow grumbled as Pierce shut the door.

Another fifteen minutes later, Willow's head was throbbing. The items on her mental to-do list, unaccustomed to being ignored for so long, seemed determined to get her attention one way or another. Even if that meant digging through her skull and breaking out of her head, which is what it felt like they were trying to do at the moment.

Had anybody gotten around to planting the rest of the clues? Would Bree think to set up a guest room for Officer Myers? Hopefully Evie had remembered to tell Antonia that there'd been a change to the guest list for dinner. And she needed to remind Pierce that three of the dinner plates from the blue china dining set were chipped, so he would need to use the red set even though it wasn't quite as nice, and—

"Ahhh," Willow groaned, cradling her throbbing head in her hands.

Do something, her head implored her. *Anything. You. Can't. Just. Sit. Here.*

Since there was nothing else to do, Willow got to her

feet and set about straightening up the office. Luckily, most of it was a mess, so she was able to kill at least half an hour by organizing errant file folders, stacking up books, and dusting off the ancient computer monitor.

Her mother had been itching to get a new computer. *It's time*, she'd said, but Willow's father had disagreed. He'd called the computer his trusty old girl and moaned about having to learn a new system. But Mrs. Ivan had been adamant. *It's time*, she'd repeated, no matter what Mr. Ivan said in response. Their last argument about it had been at breakfast on that Friday. The last morning they'd all spent together before . . .

Stay busy. You have to stay busy.

Willow backed away from the computer and sat down at the freshly decluttered desk on the other side of the tiny room. Most of the things on this desk were hers. This was where she'd done her homework, back when she'd had homework to do. There was a larger desk upstairs in her room on the fourth floor, but she'd preferred to work down here, while her father tapped away on his trusty old girl and her mother manned the front desk with Pierce. Antonia had brought snacks. Bree had helped her with the tricky math worksheets. And her mother had popped her head in when things slowed down in front to ask if she wanted a piano break—

Busy. Busy. Keep your mind busy.

There was a stack of schoolbooks on the desk. They were all from last year, and Willow wondered vaguely what the sixth-grade schoolbooks looked like. In fifth grade, she'd been required to read for thirty minutes every night, so there was also a stack of Deena Morales novels in here. She'd been rereading Mystery #13, *The Mystery of the Mountain Hall*, that Friday morning.

She'd left the book behind when she went to school, but instead of coming straight back to the Ivan afterward, she'd called her mom to ask if she could go to a friend's house. She couldn't even remember whose. Her mom had said sure, and that had been the last time she'd heard her mother's voice.

She hadn't been there when her mother collapsed in the lobby. She'd missed the 911 call, the ambulance, the paramedics, and the frantic ride to the hospital. She hadn't been there to say goodbye to her mother, and she hadn't been able to help her father. She'd missed everything.

All because she'd been off with some friend. And she couldn't even remember which friend it had been.

Stay. Busy.

She drifted to her mother's desk. Immaculate as always, it was the only part of the room that didn't need a clean-up. The surface of the desk contained a potted succulent that probably needed watering, a Hotel Ivan mug full of pens, several pieces of sheet music, and a neat stack of files.

Willow opened the top file. She braced herself for the sight of her mother's familiar, swirly handwriting. But instead, she found an official-looking typed document.

"Loan agreement," Willow read out loud, "between the Ivan family and Francisco Pierce . . . wait, what?"

Willow read farther down, skimming through the legalese until the document got to the point.

"Francisco Pierce agrees to loan the Hotel Ivan the sum of money agreed upon above, and in exchange, the Ivan family agrees to make him an equal co-owner of the Hotel Ivan . . ."

On the last page, there were spaces for two signatures: Pierce's and "a representative of the Ivan family." Both were blank. There was a sticky note next to the blank lines that read, "Talk to Pierce about this ASAP."

The note was written in her mother's swirly cursive.

There was a loud whisper from the other side of the door. "Willow! Willow! It's Evie!"

"What's going on?" Willow asked, putting the file down and throwing the door open. "Is it going OK? Is the inspector happy? It must be almost dinnertime, right? I have to be there, Evie. I can't miss—"

"We know," Evie said, then gestured to Bree, who stood

behind her holding a black top hat with a long black veil. "We have an idea! Come on!"

The Hotel Ivan's private dining room had been set with the hotel's second-finest china—the red set, Willow noted with satisfaction, not the blue one with the chipped plates. Mr. Renard was seated in the place of honor at the head of the table. Officer Myers was to his right, deep in conversation with both of the Ms. Loustrouses. Across from them sat Mr. and Mrs. Prescott and Kylie (who was still absorbed in her phone). Bree was perched in the corner, her phone in one hand, poised to film the whole dinner scene, and her Nikon in the other, to catch the occasional candid still shot.

The room was lit entirely by candles. The tiny flames bounced off the crystal chandelier, making the wineglasses sparkle mysteriously.

Behind her, someone let out a low whistle. Willow turned in the doorway and tried to hide her surprise at the sight of her father in an enormously hairy fake beard.

"It looks *beautiful* in here," Mr. Ivan breathed.

"It does," Willow agreed. She caught sight of Pierce standing at attention near the kitchen door and gave him an approving nod, exaggerating the movement so that Pierce would notice even though she was wearing a heavy veil. The unflappable concierge gave her a half smile before schooling his face back to his usual deadpan expression.

"Willow," Mr. Ivan said hesitantly, drawing her attention back to him. "I've been meaning to tell you . . . I've been thinking about what you said to me that day in the lobby. I went to my appointment with Dr. Strode."

Willow's heart leaped into her throat. She took one step back out into the hall so the guests wouldn't overhear their conversation.

"She gave me a prescription, and I've been taking it. It'll take a while, maybe a few weeks, until it fully kicks in. But I already feel a little better."

Willow squeezed her father's hand. "Dad, that's great. The best news."

Mr. Ivan squeezed her hand back. "I'm going to make things up to you, Willow. Starting now. Tonight." Then he frowned, looking over Willow's shoulder. "Where's Molly? Shouldn't she be here by now?"

"I hope she didn't forget!" Willow wrung her hands. "Go on inside, Dad, I'll go look for—"

"I'm here! I'm here!"

Mr. Ivan gave Willow's hand one last squeeze before he

disappeared into the dining room. Willow turned to ask Molly what had taken her so long, but the sight of her made Willow's breath catch in her throat.

The Headless Horsewoman—not actually headless at the moment—had traded her usual brown curls for platinum-blond locks. Her Medium robes were the brightest possible shades of pink and purple. She was standing taller than usual, teetering only slightly in her sky-high silver heels.

"You look like—" Willow's voice failed her.

"Do you think so?" Molly asked, giving a small twirl, then grabbing the wall to keep from tripping over her heels. "That's what I was going for. Leonata would have loved this whole evening."

"Yep," said Willow, fighting back tears. "She really would have."

Molly grinned.

We're going to pull this off, Willow thought to herself. And since she knew her veil fully obscured her face, she didn't fight the urge to beam with pride as she and Molly entered the dining room.

"Gentlefolk," Pierce boomed. "Please welcome Madame Zabarnathy, our Medium, and Tabitha, her mysterious veiled assistant."

There was polite applause as Molly took her place at the foot of the table, across from Mr. Renard. Willow took the seat to Molly's left, across from her father.

"Madame Zabarnathy is here to assist us in communing with the spirits," Pierce explained. "But first, Chef Antonia Fiore, the acclaimed head chef of the Hotel Ivan, is proud to present to you an exclusive five-course tasting menu. Your server tonight will be none other than Francesca Fiore, Chef Antonia's protégé and niece. Bon appétit!"

The kitchen door swung open, and Francesca came in with the first course.

Willow glanced down at the menu in front of her.

HOTEL IVAN
Menu

Vampire-Repelling Garlic Toasts

Ghost Pepper Soup

Duck Confit in a Blood Orange Sauce

Boo-Berry Tarts

A Selection of Haunted Local Cheeses

Willow grinned as she picked up her appetizer and maneuvered it up and under her veil. She took a bite, but her grin quickly faded as the tang of raw garlic burned her tongue and brought tears to her eyes.

"Oh my!" Mrs. Prescott cried out, shuddering over her own bite of toast. "Is this garlic *raw*?"

"It is!" one of the Ms. Loustrouses confirmed, setting her toast back on her plate.

"It *is*," Mr. Renard repeated from the head of the table. Willow stiffened, but the inspector finished his toast in one enormous bite, dusted off his hands, and sat back in his chair with a satisfied grin. "The raw food movement is quite trendy at the moment, isn't it? I do like a chef who isn't afraid to be avant-garde."

"Yes," Officer Myers agreed, although he pushed his appetizer plate discreetly to one side. "Avant-garde is . . . really super."

Willow, who was 100 percent certain the raw garlic had been a mistake, let out a sigh of relief as Francesca reappeared with the soup course. Her stomach growled, reminding her that she'd been so busy preparing for the inspector's visit that she'd skipped lunch. She dug into the bowl of ghost pepper soup Francesca set before her, scooped an enormous spoonful into her mouth behind her veil—

—and tried not to gag.

The soup was not just spicy. It was five-alarm, set-your-mouth-on-fire, burn-your-stomach-up-and-make-you-breathe-flames-for-days hot. Willow sputtered over her mouthful and barely forced herself to swallow. Not all the guests were as lucky; both Mr. and Mrs. Prescott spat their soup back into their bowls. One of the Ms. Loustrouses started choking, and Officer Myers pounded her industriously on the back.

Willow kicked her father under the table.

"Mhhhmmm," Mr. Ivan said quickly, still holding his first untasted bite of soup in front of his lips. "Ghost pepper soup! Not for the faint of heart!"

"I should say not," Mr. Renard agreed. Willow could

hardly bring herself to look up at the head of the table, but when she did, she saw that the inspector was licking his lips and *mmm*-ing approvingly as he brought another spoonful to his mouth. "Such flavor! Wonderful to find a chef who's not afraid to go all out with the spiciness. I find that so many celebrity chefs are afraid of heat. It's such a shame. Don't you agree, Detective Myers?"

"What? Oh, um, yes. Such a shame," Officer Myers agreed, then turned away to gulp down the entire contents of his water glass.

"I like it," said Kylie, and Willow watched incredulously as the sulky teen slurped down spoonful after spoonful, seemingly unaffected by the volcanic level of spice. Her parents also looked on in amazement.

The kitchen door opened a crack, and Willow spotted Francesca waving to get her attention.

"Excuse me," said Willow, scooting her chair back. "I, um, need to use the bathroom."

From the corner, Bree was shooting Willow questioning looks over the top of her phone. Once Willow was sure she was out of the camera's range, she spread her hands in an *I don't know* gesture before making a beeline for the kitchen.

When she pushed the swinging doors open, she found herself in the middle of a cloud of smoke.

"Francesca? What's going on?" Willow asked, fumbling to get her veil out of her eyes and struggling to be heard over the steady *beep-beep-beep* of the smoke alarm. "Francesca? Antonia? Hello?"

"Here!" A hand reached through the smoke and pulled Willow to the other side of the kitchen. "Help me!"

Francesca threw open a window and started frantically fanning cold night air into the smoke-filled kitchen. Willow opened another window and did the same until the smoke thinned out a bit and the beeping finally stopped.

Francesca slumped against the counter.

"What happened?" Willow asked, looking worriedly around the kitchen. "Where's Antonia?"

Francesca gestured vaguely to the walk-in freezer. Chef Antonia waved at Willow through the circular window in the door.

"I'm readying the crêpes Suzette!" she yelled through the metal door, which Willow noticed had been wedged shut with a broom handle. "Tell me when you're ready for the flaming sauce!" Willow jumped as the chef held up something long and metal with a flickering flame coming out one end.

"Crêpes Suzette?" Willow asked. "That's not on the menu, is it?"

"Aunt Antonia, I told you to *put the flambé torch down*!" Francesca yelled. Then, more quietly, she said, "No, it's not on the menu. She's lost it, Willow! I locked her in the freezer so she couldn't set anything else on fire."

Willow put a shocked hand to her mouth.

"It's the Fading," Francesca said defensively. "She doesn't know what she's doing."

"How did she get so bad?"

"I don't know! Everything seemed fine. Then I noticed that she hadn't roasted the garlic."

"And the soup?" Willow asked, shuddering slightly at the memory.

"That was my fault. I had no idea how many peppers to add. She keeps all of her recipes in her head, you know! And her head isn't exactly the tidiest of places these days."

"What about the rest of the dinner?" Willow asked.

Francesca wiped her sweaty forehead on her apron.

"I made all of the tarts earlier today," she said, pointing to a tower of pastries safely on the other side of the room. "So dessert should be okay."

"And the main course?" Willow asked. "The duck?"

"Incinerated," Francesca reported, gesturing to the ovens, all of which were still smoking slightly. "That's why I called you in here. What are we going to do, Willow? We have nothing to serve for the main course!"

"Crêpes Suzette!" Antonia yelled from the freezer, and Francesca let out a small shriek as a fireball exploded in the window. "Wheeeeeee!"

Willow looked wildly around the kitchen and a wave of panic rushed over her. Other than a giant saucepan, which was bubbling like mad and occasionally sending splatters of sticky orange goo (the blood orange sauce, she presumed) into the air, there was nothing.

"We have to have *something* . . ."

"We don't!" Francesca spread her hands. "The refrigerators shorted out again. The pantry's been picked clean, and the vegetable guy didn't show up this morning—"

"There's got to be something!" Willow interrupted. Then she had a sudden flash of inspiration. "Lasagna!"

"*What?*"

"There's always lasagna," Willow said desperately. "Isn't there?"

Francesca frowned. "Aunt Antonia made some last week and froze them—last week's show was about make-ahead meals—but Willow, we can't serve *lasagna*! The inspector's expecting a gourmet meal! Plus, it's frozen solid."

"We don't have a choice!" Willow insisted. "It's that or nothing."

Francesca bit her lip, thought for a minute, then nodded resolutely.

"OK," she said, shooing Willow toward the kitchen door. "I think I can make this work. Go back out there."

"What are you going to do?" Willow asked as Francesca picked up a large pot lid and held it out in front of her like a shield.

"What we always do when something goes wrong in the kitchen," Francesca said grimly, squatting down into a runner's starting stance. "Put it in a nice dish, give it a fancy name, and hope nobody notices."

She turned toward the freezer. "Aunt Antonia, *put the torch down*! I'm coming in for the lasagnas!"

Ten minutes later, Willow looked up nervously as Francesca wheeled in a tea cart with the Hotel Ivan's largest serving dish on top. She handed Pierce a notecard.

"Gentlefolk, we've had a last-minute change to the menu," Pierce announced, squinting at the card. "The duck was, regrettably, not up to Chef Antonia Fiore's exacting standards. As an alternative, she has prepared for you one of her, er, *signature* dishes. One that has been passed down through her family for generations: chilled Italian ragout with sauce tomate."

Francesca began scooping the contents of the serving dish into bowls, and Pierce helped set them in front of the hungry diners. There was complete silence at the table as the guests dug into the main course, and Willow was sure that if it were possible to die of dread, she would have turned into a ghost right then and there. Any moment now, everyone would figure out that they were eating not-quite-thawed lasagna that had been chopped up and put into fancy bowls.

Willow braced herself for the outrage. Who would

be the first to point it out? Mr. Renard? One of the Ms. Loustrouses?

But nobody said anything. Instead, she was surrounded by the sounds of chewing.

"I've always been a fan of rustic, regional dishes," Mr. Renard remarked to Officer Myers, who was nodding enthusiastically.

"Such a wonderful sauce," one of the Ms. Loustrouses added.

Stunned, Willow brought her fork up underneath her veil and tried a bite. It was Antonia's lasagna, all right. A little bit colder than usual, but still delicious. It wasn't fancy, and it wasn't gourmet, not by a long shot. But it was good. Undeniably delicious.

The conversation around the table turned to the murder mystery clues the guests had gathered earlier in the day. Willow took another bite of chilled lasagna and started to allow herself to believe once again that maybe, in spite of everything, they were going to get away with this.

She was about to turn to Molly and ask if Madame Zabernathy was ready to channel the spirits when a spirit wandered in unbidden.

Willow's mother glided through the closed dining room door, right behind Mr. Renard's chair.

Willow spat a bite of noodle into her veil.

Mrs. Ivan was looking around the room, but not in that lost way she'd been searching rooms lately. Her gaze was pointed, focused. It landed right on Willow, piercing directly through her big black hat and veil.

Willow's stomach dropped to her knees.

"*Willow Ivan*," her mother thundered. *"You've got some explaining to do!"*

CHAPTER 18
EVIE

From her hiding place outside the dining room door, Evie had seen Willow's mother coming. She hadn't properly met Mrs. Ivan before—she'd only seen her once, during her incident with the tea trolley—but she knew a thing or two about mothers. Deceased ones, even.

Specifically, she knew that when one was clenching her jaw in the way that Mrs. Ivan was, nothing good was about to happen.

She'd peered as far around the door as she'd dared and tried to signal Willow, but she could barely see her on the other side of the room. And because of that black veil, she'd had no idea whether Willow could see *her* at all.

Judging by the way Willow jumped when her mother entered the room, she hadn't noticed Evie's warning.

"Mom?" Willow asked hesitantly. Then, apparently

forgetting she was supposed to be a "mysterious veiled assistant," she climbed nervously to her feet and pulled back her veil. "Mom! You . . . you're you?"

"Of course I'm me!" the ghost snapped, hands on her hips. "Don't change the subject. I want to know why—"

"Mom," Willow interrupted, looking nervously around the table. The entire dinner party suddenly looked terribly uncomfortable, especially Mr. Ivan, who was staring at his deceased wife in much the same way Willow was. "Maybe we could talk in the lob—"

"No," Mrs. Ivan said flatly. "Nobody is leaving this room until you tell me *why you haven't been to school in six months.*"

Evie saw Willow's jaw drop and watched helplessly as all of their careful preparation went to pieces.

"*Mom,*" Willow growled with a meaningful glance down the table at Mr. Renard. "We have *guests.*"

"Only one thing comes before guests, Willow," said Mrs. Ivan, "and that's family. Why haven't you been in school?"

"I—" Willow began, but Officer Myers was scratching his head.

"Willow?" he muttered, turning to Pierce. "*This* is Willow Ivan? I thought she was out of town?"

Mr. Ivan was still staring at his wife. "Six months?" he asked her. "How do you—"

"There was a truancy notice on top of the mail stack," Mrs. Ivan informed him.

"You've been looking at the mail?" Willow ventured. Evie thought she sounded oddly glad about this.

Willow's father stood up from his chair. "What do you mean you haven't been to school in six months?" he bellowed at his daughter.

"And that—" Officer Myers squinted, and Evie could practically see the pieces of the puzzle coming together in his head. "That's Mr. Ivan?"

"Of course I haven't been in school!" Willow snapped at Mr. Ivan, and the hurt expression on her face made Evie's heart clench. "Somebody had to be here, running things. It's been *me*. All day, every day, for *months* now. Do you really mean you *didn't notice?*"

Evie couldn't see Willow's father's face, but she saw his shoulders slump.

"You *both* have a lot of explaining to do," Mrs. Ivan said icily.

Officer Myers stood up. "Yes, I should say they do. Mr. Ivan, you're under arrest."

"What?" Willow screeched. "For what?"

"Lying to a police officer, contributing to the delinquency of a minor, aiding and abetting truancy—take your pick." Officer Myers made his way deliberately toward Mr.

Ivan, even as Molly jumped up from her place at the table and planted herself between them.

Officer Myers looked affronted. "If I have to, I'll walk right through you, madam," he assured the Horsewoman. "This is not your concern."

"Of course it is!" Molly said through clenched teeth, holding her ground and adjusting her head to sit more firmly atop her shoulders.

"Wait a minute." Mr. Renard stood as well, looking confused. "Do you mean that you're a *real police officer*? This isn't a part of the show?"

"Mr. Renard," Pierce spoke up. "Perhaps this would be a good time to take you on a tour of the kitchens?"

Mr. Renard looked at Pierce as though the concierge had gone insane. Officer Myers and Molly remained squared off in front of a wide-eyed Mr. Ivan. The Ms. Loustrouses and Mr. and Mrs. Prescott all looked confused, as did Kylie. Bree, no longer filming, had lowered her phone. Across the table, Willow was looking frantically around the room.

And suddenly, Evie knew *exactly* what to do.

She closed her eyes and called up a sharp, cold wind. It flew through the room, wrapped itself around the table, and lifted the hair of everyone Living who was sitting or standing around it.

"What's that?" shrieked one of the Ms. Loustrouses.

"It's a Phantasm!" Willow shouted gratefully.

"Not now, surely," said Mr. Renard, looking uncertain. "Perhaps I should call my office—"

"It's too late," Willow said ominously. "She's here."

Evie posed dramatically in the doorway, allowing her wind to lick the edges of her black cloak.

There was a collective drawing-in of breath from around the table.

Bree raised her phone in Evie's direction.

"A Phantasm!" Officer Myers muttered wonderingly.

"We've disturbed her," Willow explained, and Evie locked eyes with Officer Myers, keeping his attention on her, allowing Willow to gesture frantically to her father.

Mr. Ivan caught the hint and started tiptoeing toward the door to the kitchen.

"*You have disturbed me,*" Evie whispered ominously.

"We're sorry!" Officer Myers squeaked.

Evie gave him a devious grin, then launched herself into the air. She did a quick circle of the room, flying right above everybody's heads, whipping up the wind as she went.

Kylie screamed.

Mr. Prescott fainted. He collapsed backward into the tea trolley, knocking it over and sending the fancy tureen holding the leftover chilled Italian ragout with sauce tomate crashing to the floor.

Mr. Ivan escaped through the kitchen door with Mrs. Ivan gliding angrily after him.

Evie, hovering now over the center of the table, felt satisfaction bubbling up inside her. The room was *hers*; every (open) eye in it was on her. Every soul, Living and dead, was watching her in rapt silence. Waiting to see what she would do next.

This was exactly how she'd always imagined doing her act in front of a crowd would feel like.

She was dizzy with joy. It was a struggle to maintain the terrifying expression on her face—a beautiful, wonderful struggle she would gladly endure for the rest of her death.

"What—what's it doing?" Mr. Renard asked shakily.

"She's going to scream!" Mrs. Prescott answered, stepping over her unconscious husband and wrapping her arms around her daughter, pulling her farther away from the table.

Evie threw her head back. Before she unleashed the Phantasm cry that she knew would bring down the house, she paused, letting the tension build for a few seconds longer. Letting herself enjoy the moment. She wanted to commit to memory every beat of terrified silence, every bit of—

—laughter?

They were laughing. They were *all* laughing.

Confused, Evie looked around the room. Mr. Renard and Officer Myers were both guffawing so hard they were holding each other up. Mrs. Prescott and Kylie were cackling. The Ms. Loustrouses were wiping their streaming eyes and hiccupping with mirth.

Bree lowered her phone again.

Willow, the only one besides Bree who wasn't laughing, pointed to the large mirror that was hanging on the wall to Evie's left.

The girl in the mirror was wearing a black Phantasm cloak and a befuddled expression. She also had long furry bunny ears, a tiny twitching bunny nose, whiskers, and a poofy cotton tail. In the corner behind her, a girl in a ruffly

pink dress was pointing at her and laughing along with the others.

They'd laugh at you, she'd said.

And Louise had made sure they did.

Evie, who'd been floating a few inches above the table, lowered herself to the floor as the dining room burst into thunderous applause.

"Greetings from the Hauntery!" her cousin hissed to Willow under the cover of all the applause.

"The—the Hauntery?" Willow whispered.

Louise turned to Evie. Evie felt her hair spring up into pigtails. She felt the whisper of ribbons against her cheeks. She didn't have to look down to know that she was now wearing the dreaded pink dress.

"That's where Evie *really* works," Louise informed Willow. "She's nothing but a Spooky Little Girl."

"Evie?" Willow ventured. "Is that true?"

Evie stared at the ground. She couldn't think. The clapping was still going on—on and on and on, not stopping even when Francesca came through the kitchen door holding a tray of tarts.

"See you at home!" Louise trilled before melting through the nearest wall.

Unable to look at Willow, Evie wedged herself into the nearest corner.

Francesca set the tray on the table, right in front of Mr. Renard.

"Capital!" Mr. Renard was shouting, still applauding. "In all my years of inspecting haunted hotels, I've never had an evening end with *comedy*. How wonderful!"

Willow took a hesitant step forward. "You—you liked it?"

"Capital evening all around!" Mr. Renard pronounced as he picked up one of the tarts and stuffed the entire thing into his mouth. He chewed away happily for several moments, until a look of horror crossed his face.

"Wuff—" he muttered through a mouthful of pastry. "Wuff ifff this?"

Pierce cleared his throat. "That is a blueberry tart, sir."

Mr. Renard immediately spewed the half-masticated tart out onto the table. *"I'm—"* he gasped, clasping his hands to his throat. *"Allergic. To. Blueberries."*

Then the hotel inspector stumbled to the side of the table and tripped over the fallen tea trolley. He collapsed onto the floor, where his head landed with a loud *splat* right in a large puddle of chilled Italian ragout with sauce tomate.

CHAPTER 19
WILLOW

Willow refreshed the *Zagged* site once, twice—

"It's up," she announced.

"Already?" Pierce asked, coming to look over her shoulder. "I wouldn't have thought Mr. Renard would be out of the hospital yet."

Willow shrugged.

It had been ten hours since the ambulance had arrived to take Mr. Renard—who was already conscious and breathing again, thanks to the EpiPen Officer Myers had jammed into his thigh—to the hospital. To add insult to injury, Mr. Renard's fall into the "chilled Italian ragout" and the resulting kerfuffle had caused the hotel inspector's blond curls (a wig, as it turned out) to come loose from his head. Willow was certain she would never forget the sight of Mr. Renard being wheeled out of Hotel Ivan on a gurney, wig clutched angrily in one fist and sauce tomate smeared all over his bald head.

Officer Myers had left as well in order to give the ambulance a police escort, but he had promised to come back in the morning "to sort out the truancy business." After the rest of the guests had departed and the mess in the dining room had been cleaned up, the Hotel Ivan had fallen strangely silent. Like a condemned prisoner awaiting her fate.

"Is it as bad as we thought it would be?" Pierce inquired.

"Worse," Willow assured him, turning the computer monitor so he could see it.

Pierce narrowed his eyes at the article and began to read out loud.

"The evening began with a tolerably entertaining whodunit-style murder mystery. The dinner contained several memorable, creative courses—

"Well, that's not so bad," Pierce said hopefully.

"Keep reading," Willow said grimly.

"But unfortunately, all of that was upstaged by management's complete disregard of this guest's food allergies, which I disclosed in writing to the head chef prior to my stay. It was only due to the quick actions of a law enforcement officer—who happened to be present at the hotel for unrelated but equally concerning reasons—that I survived the evening.

"If it were up to this hotel inspector, no establishment displaying this appalling lack of concern for the health and safety of its guests should be allowed to remain in business. Readers are advised to stay at the Hotel Ivan at their peril.

"Oh," Pierce said dismally. "Well, you did say you wanted to make the Ivan scarier."

"I didn't want to make us a health hazard!" Willow exclaimed, getting up from her chair and heading back toward the lobby. "It's over."

There was a large package wrapped in brown paper sitting on the front desk.

"What's that?" Willow asked.

"Someone from the *Zagged Guide* just dropped it off," Pierce answered. "I—I thought you should be the one to open it."

Willow ripped off the brown paper, revealing a large wooden plaque.

"It's over," Willow said again. "We're through."

THE HOTEL IVAN

MERCER STREET, VERMONT REGION

OFFICAL ZAGGED RATING:

#2

(AND THAT'S BEING GENEROUS)

Pierce didn't argue. Willow just stood there, holding the plaque, not sure whether she should throw it as hard as she could against the wall or use Antonia's flambé torch to set it on fire. Before she could decide, she caught sight of Evie making her way cautiously into the lobby.

"*You!*" Willow said accusingly. "How dare you show your face here? You—you *traitor*!"

"Willow—" Evie tried.

"How could you not tell me you worked for the Hauntery? You've been sabotaging us from the beginning!"

"*No!* I haven't! I—"

"Liar!" Willow exploded, gripping the plaque hard. "It was all lies, wasn't it? Meeting me at the library? Pretending to like the Deena Morales Mysteries? It was all so you could get inside our hotel and ruin our chances with the inspector!"

"You've got it all wrong, Willow! I wasn't—"

"Oh, really?" Willow asked icily. "So, you don't work for the Hauntery?"

"I *do*, but—"

"That's all I need to know."

"It *isn't*. What happened at the dinner—that was all my cousin's fault. She hates me, you see. She—"

"Do you think I care about your family drama?" Willow exploded. "This is about *my* family. A family I let you into! I trusted you! You were supposed to help me keep Pierce and Antonia and everybody from Fading!"

"Willow—" Pierce tried as Cuddles ran between the two girls and started barking.

"No, Pierce, you were right. She *was* hiding something. And we should have just been ourselves. I shouldn't have listened to this . . . this lying snake!"

"I was trying to help!" Evie insisted as Cuddles continued to bark. "I didn't tell you about the Hauntery at first because you hated Haunteries, and I couldn't tell you later because—"

"Shut up!" Willow screamed. And threw the plaque directly at Evie.

Evie raised her hands to protect herself.

The plaque went right through her and landed with a clatter on the lobby floor.

Evie lowered her hands and stared at Willow, wide-eyed with shock.

"*Get out of here,*" Willow said dangerously. "Go back to the Hauntery, where you belong."

Willow thought she saw Evie's lower lip wobble as she turned to go. The sight made something in Willow's stomach ache. Which, in turn, made her even more angry.

"You're pathetic, Evie MacNeil!" she shouted at Evie's retreating back. "You're just a stupid little girl who thinks she's a Phantasm!"

Evie stopped with one foot out the door. "*I'm* pathetic?" she whispered in her best menacing Phantasm voice. "Look at you, Willow Ivan. You're not even dead, but you have a library full of books you never read and a piano you never play. I would give anything for those things. But you have them, not me, and you ignore them. All you want to do is hide behind your ghosts and skulk around your haunted hotel. You moan about 'saving your ghosts.' But really? It's obvious to everyone that they don't need you to save them. You need them to save *you*."

Willow flinched. Pierce, who had caught Cuddles and was trying to keep him quiet, was staring between them, open-mouthed, as though he were watching a tennis match.

"Go back to the Hauntery," Willow told Evie. "You're not wanted here."

Then she turned on her heel and marched out of the lobby.

CHAPTER 20
EVIE

Pierce, with Cuddles in tow, hurried after Willow.

Evie stood fuming in the doorway of the lobby, unsure of exactly what to do.

She should leave. That's what Willow had told her do. She should go back to the Hauntery before anybody realized she was missing. Back to the number-one haunted hotel.

But she couldn't make her feet move. She was still working on it when Bree walked in.

"You probably shouldn't talk to me," Evie advised her. "I've been fired."

"I heard." Bree drew in a breath. "Are you a spy?"

Evie shook her head. "I do work for the Hauntery," she admitted. "But I'm not a spy. I wanted the Ivan to win."

Bree nodded, to Evie's relief. She seemed to believe her.

"I never belonged at the Hauntery," Evie continued, leaving the doorway and walking farther into the lobby. "I thought maybe I could belong here. With all of you. But I guess I was wrong."

"I don't think you were wrong," Bree said consolingly. "I think Willow is."

"Wrong for firing me?"

"Wrong for blaming you."

"Thanks, Bree. I appreciate that. But it *is* my fault. Well, mine and the blueberries'."

"You sure about that? Because I smell a rat," Bree said, walking over to where Willow had thrown the plaque. "That review came out awfully fast. And this?" She picked up the plaque and studied it carefully. "It's already got the Ivan's name on it. How could they have made this so quickly if they hadn't known ahead of time that they were going to rank us number two? And in such a mean way too, with this 'and that's being generous' nonsense?"

Evie felt the gears of her brain starting to turn. "So, you're saying the inspector already knew how he was going to rank us? Even before he showed up?"

Bree nodded. "I think he was just looking for something to hang his decision on. If it hadn't been the blueberries, it would have been something else."

"Blueberries," Evie muttered. The word kept sticking in her head for some reason. Along with an image of Mr. Renard's bald head after his wig had fallen off. "Who would have thought? I mean, who's allergic to blueberries? It's got be one of the rarest—"

She stopped dead.

"It's a shame," Bree said glumly, glancing down at her phone. "We were just starting to pick up a lot of social media traffic. I guess if this really is the end, I should just shut it all down—"

"*No!*" Evie exclaimed, bolting back toward the front door. "Don't shut it down! Not yet. You've got to buy me a little time, OK?"

"OK, but—Evie, *what are you doing?*" Bree called after her.

"Exactly what Willow told me to do. I'm going back to the Hauntery."

Evie sneaked around the back of the Hauntery until she was standing beneath the large window that overlooked the gazebo. When she stood on tiptoe, she could see that Mr. Fox's office was dark. It also seemed empty, but she couldn't see through the thick blinds.

She took one deep breath, then stepped through the wall of the hotel.

The leather journal was in the same place on Mr. Fox's desk as before, but it was closed this time. She paid it no mind and walked right through the desk until she was standing in front of the bookshelf where the one photograph was displayed. She was peering at it so intently that she didn't hear the office door swing open.

She didn't look up until Mr. Fox turned on the light.

"Ah, Ms. MacNeil. I was wondering if I'd be seeing you today."

Evie stared at him. She could practically feel her dislike of him oozing out of her every pore.

Mr. Fox pulled the *Handbook* out of his back pocket and placed it on the desk beside the journal.

"I suppose I don't need to tell you that working for a competing hotel violates the terms of your employment agreement, do I?"

"And I suppose I don't need to ask who told you about that," Evie retorted, turning back to the photograph.

"Louise has proven herself to be a very valuable asset to the Hauntery Corporation," Mr. Fox informed her. "Her position is secure. But I'm afraid that you and your parents have all been fired. And given what I heard happened at the

Hotel Ivan last night, I shan't think that you or any other souls shall be working there much longer, either."

He grinned widely at this.

Evie grinned, too, but not for the same reason. "Was it Louise who told you about the dinner?" she asked. "Or was it *your brother*?"

Evie pointed triumphantly at the framed photo. The one of Mr. Fox with his arm around another tall, bald man—a man whom Evie hadn't recognized the two times she'd met him, because she'd been so distracted by his blond curls. Until they'd fallen off into a puddle of sauce tomate on the Hotel Ivan's dining room floor.

Mr. Fox's eyes went wide.

"Blueberries," Evie told him before he could ask. "The inspector is allergic to blueberries, like you." She turned to squint at the picture again. "I should have figured it out when I saw you two together at the Hauntery. The wig threw me off. You really are almost identical, aren't you? Are you twins? Or just brothers?"

"Ms. MacNeil—"

"You said your entire family was allergic to blueberries. He could be a cousin, for all I know—it doesn't really matter. Related is related. I wonder if the *Zagged Guide* knows that their senior hotel inspector is related to the Hauntery's vice president of quality control?"

Mr. Fox did not respond.

"That explains why all non-Hauntery hotels he visits receive such poor reviews in *Zagged* while the Haunteries all get raves. Then again, he's only one reviewer . . ." Evie paused, thinking out loud. "You must have other people working inside *Zagged*, altering reviews, making sure that especially bad ones mysteriously never show up on the website. Like the one Willow left after she visited here. It must be enormously complicated, manipulating an entire organization like that . . ."

Evie trailed off, hoping Mr. Fox would take the bait and confirm her suspicions by bragging about his evil plan.

He looked tempted. He was giving her one of his patented cold stares, but the right corner of his mouth was starting to twitch.

Evie snapped her fingers.

"Oh, I see," she said, then gave him a sympathetic smile. "It was probably your brother who thought up the plan. Or maybe Corporate. You're just going along with it."

Mr. Fox finally smiled. "My brother couldn't plan his way out of a cardboard box, Ms. MacNeil. And neither could Corporate. *I* am the brains behind this operation. *I* was the one who got him a job at *Zagged* under an assumed name. *I* was the one who figured out which *Zagged* employees to bribe so that the reviews always favored Haunteries. *I* was the one who managed to keep the whole thing secret from everyone except a few select individuals at Corporate. Even his wig was *my* idea, so no one would notice the resemblance between us. You have *no* idea how deep this conspiracy goes."

"I think I do," Evie argued. "I know about the Fading. About ghosts like Patricia who Fade, but who you say have been 'transferred.' Is the Hauntery covering that up, too?"

"Of course. *Hauntery ghosts never Fade* was my idea as well."

"You made everyone believe a lie!"

"I did." Mr. Fox was smiling freely now, smug about

his own evil brilliance. "Of course Hauntery ghosts Fade. All ghosts do. It takes a bit of doing to keep up the ruse of transferring them, but no one said being vice president of quality control was easy. That's where Professor Torrance came in."

"The scientist?" Evie asked. "The one who proved that fear keeps ghosts from Fading?"

"Professor Torrance was paid by the Hauntery, of course. Fear has nothing to do with it, at least as far as we can tell. But we can't let the ghosts know that. We'd never get decent staff if they knew the truth."

"They will know," Evie said darkly. "I'm going to tell everyone."

Mr. Fox's grin turned nasty. "And who do you think would believe you? You're nothing but a disgruntled ex-employee. A little girl. A *dead* little girl. With no proof."

"I—" Evie paused and eyed the picture frame.

Mr. Fox laughed. "Far too young to manipulate objects, aren't you? It'll be your word against mine. How do you think that'll go?"

Evie didn't answer. Her fingers twitched. The picture frame was so close . . . so close . . .

Mr. Fox sighed and leaned against the far side of the desk. "It's a shame, really. You had such a good thing going for yourself and your family. All you had to do was stay in your place. Do as you were told. Smile. Giggle. Spout out tiny snippets of adorable ad-lib . . ."

Evie felt her upper lip curl into a sneer. She thought about what Bree had said:

Nobody's going to believe it for *you.*

Mr. Fox tapped the *Handbook.* "It was all here, laid out for you by your betters. But you had to go and try to prove us wrong. How's that going for you, little girl? Huh?"

Evie surged forward and snatched the picture frame off the shelf.

Her hands trembled for a moment, and she nearly dropped it. The frame wobbled. But then she felt the solid weight of it, allowed her fingertips to feel the grooves in the cool, smooth metal. She was doing it—she was *holding* it. Every bit as solidly as she had ever held anything when she was alive.

She looked up at Mr. Fox. "How's it going?" she repeated, pretended to consider his question. "Pretty well, actually. Thank you for asking."

Mr. Fox's jaw dropped.

Evie used his moment of hesitation to move behind the desk, being sure to keep it between them. Then she casually leaned over and picked up the journal. It felt solid in her hand, too. Heavy with the weight of the proof it held. A record of all the Faded Hauntery ghosts.

"What's the matter, Mr. Fox?" Evie asked icily as a slight wind kicked up around them. "Did I forget to smile?"

Mr. Fox's face turned purple with rage. He opened and closed his mouth as though he were trying to speak but couldn't find the words. He looked around nervously, trying to figure out where the wind was coming from.

"I guess I forgot to giggle," Evie said as the temperature in the room dropped abruptly.

She sprang up on top of the desk. When her feet hit the wood surface, she didn't hesitate; she threw her head back and let out the loudest, deepest, most bone-chilling Phantasm cry she had ever uttered. The one she had meant to do at the dinner party before Louise had ruined it. She'd been looking forward to the reaction that a room full of people would have to the sound, but seeing Mr. Fox's reaction was even sweeter.

His face instantly went from purple to sheet white. He seemed to forget how to stand up properly, and he tripped over his own feet twice as he scrambled backward toward the office door. Once he finally made it there, he fumbled behind his back for the doorknob, trembling all over, unable to take his eyes off of Evie.

With a small sigh of satisfaction, Evie hopped down from the desk. Clutching the picture frame and the journal to her chest, she walked purposefully toward the office door.

"Out of my way," she growled, "before I yell again."

After two more panicked attempts, Mr. Fox finally managed to get the doorknob working properly. He opened the door and stumbled through it, throwing one last terrified glance in Evie's direction before running headlong down the hallway.

Evie walked grandly through the open door and smiled at the fleeing vice president of quality control.

"How about *that* for 'adorable ad-lib'?"

CHAPTER 21
WILLOW

Willow waited until she was sure Evie was gone before she went back to the lobby. When she did return, she was shocked to find her mother there, floating behind the front desk.

"Mom!" Willow exclaimed, gulping as her mother flashed in and out of focus. At times, she could only see her thin, transparent outline. "You're—you're—"

"Fading," her mother finished. "Yes."

"But—*no*! You were just starting to get back to normal!"

"I'm a WISP, Willow."

"No, you're not! You can't be, you—"

"Willow, please. I think this might be my Last Gasp. We need to talk. And I don't know how much longer I have. Walk with me. Please?"

Without waiting for an answer, Willow's mother drifted through the lobby. Willow ran to catch up.

"I just had a long conversation with your father," she said.

"Is he—"

"He's gone to the police station to deal with the truancy business," she said, giving Willow a very deliberate look. Then her frown softened. "He told me about Anna. And about Leo and Alford."

Willow swallowed. "It's all my fault, Mom. I've done everything wrong."

"Willow—"

"I trusted that wannabe Phantasm. I was trying to do something special for the inspector. Something exciting! And scary!"

"Scary? Why?"

"So that everybody would stop Fading! That scientist, that Professor Torrance guy, says that ghosts need to inspire fear to stay on this plane. And we were losing all of our business to the Hauntery, and . . . I've made a mess of everything, haven't I?"

"I wouldn't say that," Willow's mother said, turning slightly to make her way down the first-floor hallway. "It sounds to me like you've been working very hard. Your heart is in the right place. But the Hotel Ivan has never been about scaring people. It's about service, and family, and fun. Never fear. We've had our ghosts for centuries longer than any Hauntery. Why do you think that is?"

"I don't know," Willow grumbled.

Willow's mother paused beneath the portrait of Gracey Ivan. "Our family has always been a little quirky," she said, smiling up at the Hotel Ivan's legendary founder. "Starting with Gracey. We've been explorers. We've been writers. Scientists. Inventors."

"Musicians," Willow added, thinking of her mother at the piano.

"Plus, there was the bank robber. And a gambler. And I know he's not technically an Ivan, but I'm almost positive that Pierce was a pirate while he was Living, if you can imagine that!" her mother added with a laugh. "Whatever else you can say about the Ivans, you've got to admit that we know how to *live*. I don't know about all of this fear business—that feels cooked up to me. As long as there's been a Living Ivan in this hotel, our ghosts have gotten along fine."

Willow hesitated. "What about me, then? I'm a Living Ivan, and I haven't been able to stop them from Fading."

"Yes, you are alive," Willow's mother said carefully. "But have you really been *living*, Willow?"

"Of course I have!"

Her mother raised an eyebrow. "Name one thing you've

done in the past six months." And when Willow opened her mouth, she added, "Something that has nothing to do with the running of this hotel."

"I—" Willow stopped to think for a moment. The last six months had been an endless cycle of linen deliveries, taking reservations, checking guests in, checking guests out, dealing with complaints . . .

"I went to the library!" she remembered suddenly. Then she shuddered. "I met Evie."

"Yes," Willow's mother said, stopping beneath the most recent portrait, that of Willow's grandmother. "You've been working so hard, night and day, for months now. You've been working, and grieving, and worrying. Your father— well, he's been no better, and I know he's been no help to you. He finally saw a doctor, though, and went back on his medication. And you started visiting the library, where you made a friend. It's no coincidence that once both of those things happened, I started being able to see things clearly. I think they were what pushed me toward my Last Gasp."

Willow shook her head. "I don't understand."

"I think you do."

Willow frowned and looked up at the portraits. All of those Ivans. The Ivans who had been so much, done so much . . .

"Dad and I are Living, but we haven't been acting like it," Willow said carefully, flinching at a memory of Evie shouting, *All you want to do is hide behind your ghosts and skulk around your haunted hotel.* "You don't think it's fear that keeps ghosts from Fading. You think it's being close to Living people who . . . who are really living?"

Willow's mother nodded.

"But I've been working so hard!" Willow protested. "These past few months, I've been busier than ever! I've barely slept! I've been—"

"Skipping school."

"Well, yes. I had too much to do here."

"And your piano lessons?"

"I tried to keep those up, but they conflicted with too many staff meetings—"

"Your friends from school? When was the last time you spoke to someone your own age?"

"Well, there's Evie—"

"Someone your own age who doesn't work at this hotel?"

Willow opened her mouth, and then shut it again and sat down hard on a nearby bench. That couldn't be the answer. It couldn't be that everything she'd done to try to help had actually been hurting them. It couldn't be . . .

Could it?

"So it *is* my fault?" Willow asked, fighting back tears.

"Everything I've been doing, it's been making them all Fade even faster?"

Her mother knelt down in front of her. "No, sweetheart. Fading isn't as simple as that. For all the theories out there, even mine, nobody *really* knows how Fading works. Or why some people come back as ghosts and some don't. Or why some, like me, come back as WISPs while others take centuries to Fade. And you know what? Maybe that's okay. Life's always been a bit of a mystery. Why shouldn't death be?"

"So, it *wasn't* my fault that Leo and Alford Faded? Or Anna?"

"Anna started Fading well before the Ivan's financial troubles started. And Leo and Alford had been winding down for the last decade or so. They were ready to Move On. Alford didn't expect them to make it to this year. They *chose* to go. Somehow, they knew they were ready. It wasn't your fault."

Willow nodded. She felt lighter all of a sudden. As though a heavy weight had been lifted from her heart.

"But," her mother continued ominously, and a tiny bit of the weight returned, "for all of your hard work, my love, you haven't been acting much like an Ivan lately."

"What are you *talking* about?" Willow exclaimed. "I've been running the hotel! Practically by myself! The Ivans have been running this hotel for four hundred years. It's what we do!"

"Yes," said Mrs. Ivan gently. "It *is* what we do. But we've never done it alone."

"What?" Willow asked, confused.

Her mother reached up as though to touch Willow's face, but stopped just short of her cheek.

"You've taken on so much these past months. But you can't be the housekeeper, the front desk manager, the plumber, the accountant, and the event planner all at the same time. You can't do everything yourself, and you can't expect to control everything. You need to let people help you. We all need a little bit of help sometimes. Look at your father—he's getting the help he needs now, thanks to you. But I can't Move On until I know that you're doing the same."

Willow's eyes filled with tears.

"The Ivan was having financial trouble before I died," Mrs. Ivan admitted. "Well before the Hauntery came to town. My plan was to ask Pierce for help."

"I know," Willow said. "I saw the loan papers on your desk."

"Pierce has been at the Ivan since the very beginning," Mrs. Ivan said. "Far longer than any of us. It only seemed fitting to me that he become an owner. I never got the chance to ask him. But I think you should."

"What's the point?" Willow asked. "That inspector from the *Zagged Guide*—he said *awful* things, Mom. Nobody is going to want to stay here. No matter how much money Pierce lends us, no matter how nicely we fix up the Ivan, what does it matter if we don't have any guests? It's too late."

"It's *not*!"

The STAFF ONLY door flew open, and Willow and her mother both turned, startled, as Evie charged into the hallway with an armload of things—a picture frame, a big leather book, and the front desk phone.

"Evie!" Willow exclaimed. "You're . . . you're *holding*—"

"Proof! That's what I'm holding. I'll explain later. But right now . . ." Evie paused, juggling the objects in her hands until she was holding the phone out to Willow. "It's for you!"

Willow put the phone up to her ear.

"Hello?"

"Ms. Ivan? Freddy Thompson. Editor of the *Zagged Guide*. How are you this evening?"

"F-fine . . ." Willow looked up at Evie, who was grinning like a jack-o'-lantern.

"I wanted to apologize about Mr. Renard. None of

us here at *Zagged* had any idea that our most senior hotel inspector was related to one of the top executives at the Hauntery. I hope you believe that."

"R-related?" Willow asked, squinting at the photograph that Evie was holding in front of her face.

"Yes, your Phantasm emailed me the photo. Really threw us for a loop here. I can assure you Mr. Renard has been fired. His reviews have all been retracted. In fact, we are double-checking the accuracy of all of our reviews, as it appears many of them have been tampered with. We should be able to send another inspector in to review the Ivan by next week. How's Tuesday afternoon for you?"

"Tuesday? Um, sure?"

"Great. Thank you for your understanding, Ms. Ivan. We'd hate for the good relationship between *Zagged* and an esteemed Vermont institution like the Hotel Ivan to be in any way damaged by this . . . little misunderstanding. Thank you, and goodbye!"

Willow handed the phone back to a still-beaming Evie.

"How . . . ?" Willow asked her.

"It's a long story," Evie assured her. "Mostly to do with blueberries. But the bottom line is, we have another chance!"

"*We?*" Willow asked her pointedly.

"*We,*" Evie confirmed. Then she sighed. "I'm sorry I lied. I wanted to tell you about the Hauntery. I almost did a few times. But I didn't know how you'd react. I was afraid that you'd—"

"Yell at you?" Willow supplied, feeling ashamed. "Fire you? You're right. I didn't react well. I didn't even listen to you. I just . . . fired you. I'm sorry I did that."

"Oh, that," Evie said, waving her hand dismissively. "Don't worry. I know you only mean, like, ten percent of what you say when you're mad."

"That's right . . ."

"We're OK," Evie assured her. "The important thing is that the Hotel Ivan is still alive!"

"We're more than just alive!" Bree announced, rushing into the hallway behind Evie. "We're *trending.*"

"We're *what?*"

"Trending! On all platforms! I've been streaming snippets from the whodunit since yesterday," Bree explained. "And about forty-five minutes ago, somebody named Angelina Garcia mentioned us on Twitter—"

Willow's breath caught in her throat; next to her, Evie made a tiny, high-pitched noise.

"Angelina Garcia?" Willow choked out. "The author of the Deena Morales Mysteries?"

"The very same! She says, and I quote, 'Check out this

amazing haunted hotel! Exactly what I was picturing as I wrote *The Clue in the Old Inn!*'"

"Wow!" Willow and Evie both exclaimed.

"Wow is right! Ever since then our posts have been retweeted, regrammed, and shared more than fifty thousand times. She must have like two million followers!"

"Wait, Bree, did you post the part at the end?" Evie asked, her voice filled with dread. "The part where I—"

"Of course I didn't post *that*," Bree assured her. "I did a bit of editing with the last piece of footage so that it left everybody hanging. Then I said that if they wanted to know whodunit, they'd have to make a reservation to stay here and solve the crime themselves. And it worked! We've had hundreds of reservations just in the past half hour!"

"Hundreds?" Willow breathed.

"We're going to be busy," Bree said with a wink. "You'd better hire a new housekeeper, Willow. I don't think you're going to be able to do that job yourself anymore."

She went back into her office, leaving Evie and Willow staring at each other.

"We did it! And Angelina Garcia helped!" Willow turned toward her mother. "Mom, did you—"

She broke off. Mrs. Ivan was almost invisible now, and the parts Willow could see were flickering even faster than before.

"I'm going to go tell the others!" Evie enthused, not appearing to notice Mrs. Ivan's state. "We have a *lot* to do before Tuesday. We can't do the exact same mystery again, obviously, now that it's gone viral. But maybe if we just tweak the clues a bit . . ." She dashed out of the room, still planning out loud.

"She seems smart," Mrs. Ivan observed.

"Frighteningly smart," Willow muttered, then shook her head. "Mom, are you . . . ?"

"Moving On?" Mrs. Ivan asked. "Yes, I think so."

"No!"

"Willow—"

"Don't you want to stay?" she asked desperately. "If Alford and Leo could choose to go, can't you choose to stay? Don't you want to be here at the Ivan? With me?"

"Of course I *want* to stay. But I'm not like the others, Willow. I'm a WISP. I only ever had one foot in this world, and it was never going to be for long. I was never meant to be a ghost."

Willow could only shake her head.

"Your father has let me go. *I've* let go. The only one keeping me here now, Willow, is you. This is my Last Gasp."

"No!" Willow said firmly. "You're wrong. It can't be!"

Mrs. Ivan put her hand alongside Willow's cheek again, the closest she could get to touching her. "It was my fault, Willow. All of it. How could you and your father be expected to move on with your lives when I was still here, wandering the halls? Not sure of who I was or what I was doing? I can't imagine how hard that must have been for you."

"You can't go," Willow implored her. "The whole point of saving the Ivan was to save *you*!"

"Then *save me*, Willow. Save me from haunting you and keeping you from living your life. Save me from making a ghost of you. Let me go. Let me go as *me*, before I lose myself again."

Willow scrubbed the tears from her cheeks.

She'd said goodbye to her mother a hundred times in the past few months. Or she'd thought she had. At the hospital, at the funeral . . . but none of those times had been real. Not when her mother's ghost had been standing beside her the whole time. She'd gone from shock to crushing grief to numbness, and somehow, she'd gotten stuck there. She wanted to feel again. She was ready to feel again. But how could this possibly be the way?

"It's not fair," Willow pleaded.

"No, my love, it's not," her mother agreed with a small sigh. "Life almost never is."

"What about death?

"I'll let you know."

Mrs. Ivan smiled. And something inside of Willow—
something that had been clenched tight and carefully
tucked away for months now—finally let go. Her mother's
outline grew blurrier and blurrier until finally, everything
except her smile was gone.

Willow's throat closed up. Suddenly, there were a million things she wanted to say. A million things her mother
needed to hear. A million things she knew they didn't have
time for.

How do you pick the last thing you're ever going to say
to your mom?

"The piano needs tuning," Willow finally choked out.
"I'll take care of it, I promise."

The fading smile widened.

"I know you will."

And then she was gone.

CHAPTER 22
EVIE
A few months later . . .

E vie lingered outside the front gates of the Mercer Street Hauntery.

The hotel was officially closed now. In fact, in the last few months, almost one-third of all Hauntery properties worldwide had been shut down.

It had been a relatively simple matter to convince Officer Myers that the ironclad evidence Evie had stolen from Mr. Fox's office was *far* more interesting than a boring old truancy case against Mr. Ivan. Once word got out about the rigged *Zagged* reviews and the fake scientific findings of Professor Torrance (who, it turned out, wasn't really a scientist at all), the FBI ended up taking over the investigation.

But not before Officer Myers was finally able to transfer to the NCE Relations unit.

Most of the Hauntery's Corporate management, including Mr. Fox, had ended up in prison. The corporation itself, in deep financial trouble after the ensuing public relations scandal, was eventually bought by Kathleen Deetz. The ghost billionaire overhauled the entire company, closed down all of its questionably historic properties (like the one on Mercer Street), and pledged to devote herself to better working conditions for her NCE employees.

The Hauntery Corporation was now the largest ghost-owned business in the world. A lot of its NCE employees decided to stay on. But some, like Evie's parents, had decided to go elsewhere.

Evie watched as her parents walked down the front steps of the defunct hotel toward the waiting Phamazon van.

"Evie!" her mother exclaimed. "Have you changed your mind? Will you be joining us at Phamazon?"

"No," Evie replied, trying not to gag at the thought. "I told you guys, I already have a job."

"Are you *sure*?" her father pressed her. "There's still a market for Spooky Little Girl hauntings. Maybe you and Louise could patch things up and get the act back together?"

He gestured to the front door of the hotel, from which Louise had just emerged.

"No thanks," Evie said firmly. "I really just came to say goodbye."

Evie's mother and father both enveloped her in a hug.

"I can't believe we won't all be together anymore," her mother lamented. "I don't want to lose you, Evie."

"You're not losing me, Mom," Evie assured her. "I'm not upper-case Moving On. I'm lower-case moving on. To a place that's perfect for me. The Ivan is where I belong."

"It really is quite a charming hotel," Evie's mother admitted. "But if you get tired of it, just say the word! You can join us at Phamazon whenever you like."

"You know what they're saying, right?" Mr. Ivan added. Then he puffed up his chest and announced in his Phantasm voice, *"Phamazon ghosts never Fade!"*

"I'll keep that in mind," Evie promised as her parents climbed into the van.

Louise hesitated at the top of the steps, and Evie noticed that she was wearing plain jeans and a sweater. The regular clothes looked strange on her. Evie couldn't remember the last time she'd seen her cousin wearing anything other than her Spooky Little Girl dress or her internship suit.

"What?" asked Louise, noticing her staring.

"Nothing. You just look different, that's all."

"So do you. I thought you hated dresses."

Evie looked down at the blue sundress she was wearing. "I like *some* dresses," she said. "When I get to pick them for myself."

"Huh," was all Louise said.

"So, are you moving to another Hauntery?" Evie asked.

Louise shrugged. "They offered me a job at one of their other properties. But now that Mr. Fox is in prison, my internship is over. All the work I put into it is gone. I suppose that makes you happy?"

"I thought it would," Evie admitted. "I thought it would feel good to see you miserable. But it doesn't."

Louise didn't say anything to that.

"Did it feel good to you?" Evie asked her. "When you blew my cover at that dinner party?"

"No, I thought it would, but it didn't. I wish you'd told me about your job at the Ivan."

"Are you serious?" Evie asked incredulously. "If I'd told you, you would've gone running straight to Mr. Fox and gotten me in trouble!"

"No, I wouldn't have!"

Evie gave her a *look*, and Louise threw up her hands.

"All right, I probably would have. But only because you were doing better at advancing your career than I was. I was *so* jealous when I found out what you were up to."

"Jealous? Of me?" Evie squeaked, then shook her head. "I don't get you, Louise. I never have. I mean, did you actually *like* being a Spooky Little Girl? Wearing those stupid outfits? Saying our dumb lines?"

"I didn't mind it," Louise said quietly. "But I never took it as seriously as you did. For me, it was just a job. The dress was just a costume. The lines were just words I memorized. None of it ever defined me. I thought if I did it all well enough, it would lead to other things. Better jobs, better costumes. I always told you I wasn't planning to be a Spooky Little Girl forever. Why do you always have to take everything so personally?"

"I don't know," Evie said. She'd never really thought about it that way before.

Then again, Mr. Fox hadn't treated Louise the way he'd treated her. He'd always been nice to Louise, giving her compliments and advancement opportunities. Evie was willing to bet that Louise would have felt differently if Mr. Fox had told *her* that her worth was based on her ability to smile and giggle. It was hard not to take things like that personally.

Evie looked at her cousin. "Why didn't we ever talk like this before?"

Louise shrugged. "I don't know. But for what it's worth, I'm sorry I ruined your Phantasm act that night. I'm glad it didn't cost you your job."

"Thanks," Evie said. But she couldn't quite bring herself to apologize for bringing down Mr. Fox—she'd never apologize for that!

"You're a Terrifying Phantasm now, right?"

"Yep."

"Just like you wanted. *That* must feel good."

"It does," Evie said, unable to hide her smile. "It really, really does."

"Maybe one day I'll get what I want, too."

"What *do* you want, Louise?"

"I'm not sure yet," Louise mused. "For now, I'm going

to go back to school. Maybe one day I'll try to get an internship at another hotel. Or maybe not. Now that I know I don't *have* to inspire fear to keep from Fading, it seems like there are a million things I could do! I have my whole afterlife ahead of me, you know?"

"I do know," Evie said. "And I can't believe I'm saying this, but good luck, Louise."

"Good luck to you, too. Uh, Evie?"

"Yes?"

Louise sucked in a breath. "If it makes any difference, you've always been terrifying to me. I don't know why Mr. Fox couldn't see it."

Evie grinned even harder. "I'll take that as a compliment."

CHAPTER 23
WILLOW
A few months after that . . .

Willow breezed into the lobby and stashed her backpack behind the front desk.

"I'm *home!*"

Nobody answered her. Curious, she stuck her head in through the STAFF ONLY door, but the small room was empty.

"Dad?" she called uncertainly, swallowing an unwelcome feeling of dread.

"Here!" her father called, coming in from the back of the hotel. "I was just signing for the linens."

Willow let out a relieved breath. Her father bent to wipe a speck of dust off of his new shoes. They were brown leather and decked out with the ugliest leather tassels Willow had ever seen.

She couldn't stop smiling at them.

"How was school?"

"Good. I invited a few friends over after school tomorrow, if that's OK?"

"Fine by me. Are you off to your piano lesson?"

"No, that's Thursday. Today I have a shift at the front desk," Willow reminded him, settling herself on the stool.

"Are you sure?" her father asked. "I can cover it if you have homework."

"I did it all yesterday so I'd be able to enjoy this," Willow informed him. "I only get one shift a week now, remember?"

"I remember," her father said with a smile. "Well, if you really don't need me, then I'll go to my appointment with Dr. Strode . . ."

"Go ahead," Willow told him, putting both hands on top of the front desk and sighing contentedly. "I've got everything under control here."

As Willow's father left out the back door, the front door of the Ivan swung open. Willow did a double take as she recognized the family who walked in.

"The Fosters!" she chirped. "How nice to see you again. Welcome back to the Hotel Ivan."

"Thank you . . ." Mr. Foster said uncertainly.

"What can I do for you?"

"Er, well, it's the darndest thing." Mr. Foster scratched his head as Mrs. Foster and the kids went to the fireplace to greet Cuddles. "We had reservations at the Mercer Street Hauntery, but when we got there, it appeared to be . . . that is, it looked like it had been . . ."

"Shut down," Willow finished for him. "They didn't notify you?"

"Uh, no," Mr. Foster said with a frown. "They didn't tell us. I don't suppose . . ." He suddenly looked very uncomfortable. "I mean, I realize I was quite rude the last time we stayed here, and now here we are, turning up at the last minute . . ."

"Would you like a room, Mr. Foster?" Willow asked, hiding her smile.

"Yes, please! If you have one available."

"I believe I do," Willow said, consulting the brand-new flat monitor that now sat proudly on the front desk. "Yes, we had a cancellation this morning, so we have one room available. Our honeymoon suite: the Alford and Leopold Room."

"Perfect!" Mr. Foster beamed. "And I'm assuming the other activities . . . they're still the same?"

"Yes," Willow assured him. "Our resident Headless

Horsewoman is available to guide you on rides. Our chefs are even at this moment preparing a gourmet meal for dinner—"

Willow paused as an earsplitting yowl crashed through the hotel, shaking the walls.

"I'm afraid you've just missed today's Terrifying Phantasm Experience," she added as Mrs. Foster clutched her children to her in a panic. "But don't worry. Our Phantasm, Evie MacNeil, will be doing another show tomorrow. Did you hear that the Vermont Board of Tourism recently ranked her number three in the state?"

"Excellent," said Mr. Foster shakily. "We'll, um, be sure not to miss that."

One of the kids squirmed free of Mrs. Foster's grip and ran to the first-floor hallway. "Who's that?" he asked, pointing a finger at the closest portrait. The newest one, which had been hanging on the wall for less than a month.

"That's my mother," Willow answered, walking up behind him and swallowing a small lump in her throat. "She died last year. She stayed around for a little while, haunting the hotel, but then she eventually Moved On."

"Oh," the kid said. "Will *you* come back and haunt the hotel when you die?"

"Maybe. Who knows?"

"Will you be a scary ghost?"

Willow bent down so she was level with the boy's face.

"Don't tell Evie the Phantasm I said this, but between you and me, I think scary is pretty overrated."

"Totally," the kid agreed, then scampered off to follow his parents to their room.

Chefs Antonia and Francesca entered the lobby, wheeling an enormous cake between them on the tea trolley.

"Willow, are you coming?" Chef Antonia asked, gesturing toward the music room. "We're all set up for Pierce's party."

"It's not every day that one of the hotel owners turns four hundred and twenty years old!" Francesca added merrily.

Willow smiled. Pierce had been delighted when she'd shown him the paperwork she'd found on her mother's desk, and he'd immediately agreed to sign it. His only stipulation had been that a small portion of the money he loaned the Ivan be set aside to rebuild Willow's Rainy Day Fund.

Just in case.

"Pierce is going to hate this party," Antonia pointed out. "He loathes being the center of attention."

"He'll like the cake, though," Francesca pointed out. "I made it gluten free."

"Gluten free?" Chef Antonia stared at her niece in shock, then looked mournfully down at the cake. "This is my great-grandmother's recipe! How *dare* you—and Pierce isn't allergic to gluten!"

"He has a *sensitivity* to gluten," Francesca sniffed. "And it's *his* birthday, not yours—"

"I'll be right there!" Willow interrupted them. "Don't start without me! And is Bree here yet? She said she—"

"I'm here!" Bree announced, coming in through the front door. "I wouldn't miss Pierce's birthday!"

One of the biggest changes to the Hotel Ivan, and the hardest one for Willow to come to terms with, was Bree's departure. Once the Ivan was firmly back on its feet, Bree had decided the time was finally right to open her own photography business. She'd helped hire two new ghosts to replace her: a quietly efficient new officer manager named Bert (who came highly recommended on GhouledIn), and a promising new social media manager named Nadiya (who also worked part-time for Bree whenever she needed an assistant photographer).

Willow missed seeing Bree every day. But since her

new photography studio was right down the street, she still popped into the Ivan several times a week to have lunch or to check up on the new hires.

"Bree!" exclaimed Evie, coming in from the back of the hotel. She was still wearing her Phantasm outfit and lending an arm to a headless Molly, but she dropped the Headless Horsewoman's elbow in order to hug Bree. "I'm so glad you're here!"

"Me too!" Bree enthused, and then her voice turned very serious. "You're all coming to my exhibit this Saturday, right?"

There were nods all around.

"Oh, good," she said, sounding relieved. "It's my first big event. I really need it to go well!"

"We're completely booked this weekend," Willow told her, "but I think Bert can manage on his own for a few hours while the rest of us go. We wouldn't miss it!"

"Oh, Bert'll be fine," Bree said with a wink. "I trained him myself!"

"I'm making it my mission to find my head before Saturday," Molly announced. "Until then, though, would someone mind leading me to the party?"

Bree took Molly's arm.

"Come on, Cuddles," Bree said to the dog, who was running in circles around her legs. "Let's go embarrass Pierce!"

The three of them disappeared into the music room.

"Ready for cake?" Evie asked Willow.

"Almost," Willow said as she straightened up some of the knickknacks on the front desk, including the (slightly dented) wooden plaque they'd received from the *Zagged Guide*.

Evie blanched. "Ugh, can we *please* put that stupid thing away?"

"What?" Willow asked, looking at the plaque in surprise. "Why would we do that?"

"Seriously?"

"It's our official *Zagged* ranking, after all," Willow argued.

Despite the editor's assurances to Willow over the phone, the *Zagged Guide* had never sent another inspector to the Ivan. Once the company had fired Mr. Renard and every other member of staff that had been bribed by the Hauntery to rig reviews, they were left with barely enough employees to keep the publication in business. They still posted reviews from time to time, but nobody really seemed to care what the *Zagged Guide* thought of anything anymore.

Willow hadn't even bothered to remind Mr. Thompson to schedule a new inspection. Even if that meant that the Ivan was officially going to be number two forever, nobody at the hotel seemed to mind. Between the closing of the Mercer Street Hauntery and all the social media attention they'd been receiving about their whodunits, the Ivan was now booked solid through next Halloween.

Willow still wasn't sure if her mother's theory about Fading was true or not. But with all those guests coming through, as well as Willow and her father's newfound commitment to getting a life, there was more living going on at the Hotel Ivan than ever before. It might have been sheer coincidence, but Pierce's hand had rematerialized, Antonia was back to using the flambé torch only on actual flambé, and Cuddles hadn't had an accident in months.

"The plaque stays," Willow pronounced emphatically. "It reminds me of what happens when we stop being ourselves. Besides, it looks good there."

"The Living," Evie muttered, rolling her eyes. "Hey, did I tell you that Louise got into the Cornell School of Hotel Management?"

"Really?"

"Yeah. Thanks for having your dad write her that letter of recommendation."

"I was kind of surprised you wanted to help her, after everything she did."

Even now, months later, Evie still wasn't sure what to make of the conversation she'd with Louise on the day they'd moved out of the Hauntery. Or why she'd decided to help the person who had tried so hard to ruin everything for her.

She shrugged. "She's family. What are you going to do, you know?"

"I *do* know," said Willow, looking fondly toward the music room. "Oh, and I meant to tell you! We got a very interesting reservation early this morning that I thought you'd want to see."

Willow turned the computer monitor so Evie could see it, then bit back a grin when Evie's eyes nearly popped out of their sockets.

"Angelina Garcia!" Evie squealed. "Angelina Garcia's coming *here*?!"

"Yep!" Willow squealed back. "She told Pierce on the phone that she's writing a sequel to *The Clue in the Old Inn* and is counting on the Ivan to inspire her! She's booked a whodunit!"

"We've got to come up with something *amazing* for that night," Evie said with great feeling, and Willow could tell she was already thinking hard. "Something that will totally knock her socks off."

Willow grinned. "I'm sure we'll be able to think of something. Maybe—"

But before she could go on, Pierce entered the lobby.

"Pierce!" Evie exclaimed, then pretended to look shocked. "Are you sure you're four hundred and twenty years old today? You don't look a day over four hundred and nineteen!"

Pierce rolled his eyes. "Let's get this over with," he said, walking resignedly toward the music room. "There's not going to be singing, is there?"

"Probably," Willow admitted.

Pierce heaved an enormous, bracing sigh just as Bert appeared in the doorway of the lobby.

"Willow? Pierce? I'm sorry to interrupt," he said, looking uncomfortable. "The Fosters have rung down for room service, but the whole staff is in the music room for the party. I didn't know what to do . . ."

Pierce's face fell as he turned away from the music room. "We can celebrate another night," he said, as deadpan as ever.

"No!" Willow said firmly. "No, we can't. Let's go blow your candles out, Pierce. The Fosters can wait."

"Are you sure?" Pierce asked. His expression was unreadable, but Willow caught sight of a tiny bit of moisture around his eyes.

Willow nodded. "Only one thing comes before guests," she said as she led Pierce and Evie into the music room. "And that's family."

"HAPPY BIRTHDAY, PIERCE!" the room exploded.

Willow took a seat at the newly tuned piano and began to play. Everyone started dancing. At some point, somebody brought the Fosters a plate full of cake. Then there was more dancing.

And Willow couldn't help but think:

If this is second best, who would ever want to be first?

ACKNOWLEDGMENTS

For better or for worse, the curse of "being a writer" is that no matter how much time and energy you dedicate to your craft, there's always more to learn. After fourteen years in this industry and five books with my name on the cover, I'm floored by how much I still don't know. But I'm happy to say that there *are* a few things I've found to be true beyond a shadow of a doubt:

First, that I would be hopelessly lost without the wisdom and guidance of my amazing agent, Sarah LaPolla. Every writer needs a signpost in the fog, and you are mine. Thank you for having my back and always steering me in the right direction.

Second, that every book eventually finds the home it's destined to have. I'm thrilled that *The Second-Best Haunted Hotel on Mercer Street* found Abrams. Thank you to my brilliant editor, Erica Finkel, for acquiring the book (on Halloween, no less—your spooky sense of timing is just one of the many things I appreciate about you!) and for all of your help bringing Willow and Evie's story to the next level. My deepest gratitude to the whole team at Abrams, including Emily Daluga, Marie Oishi, Jenn Jimenez, Marcie Lawrence, Pam Notarantonio, Melanie Chang,

Jenny Choy, Trish McNamara O'Neill, Mary Marolla, Megan Evans, Andrew Smith, Jody Mosley, Elisa Gonzales, Wendy Ceballos, and Michael Jacobs. Thanks to the delightful copyeditor, Alison Cherry. I am also thrilled to have had the chance to work with immensely talented Jane Pica.

Third, that every writer needs a creative village. I am indescribably grateful for mine: the weird, wonderful, and extraordinarily talented folks of the Austin Kidlit community. Thank you to my ladies of the Lodge of Death; to the wonderful Cynthia Leitich Smith (and our always-epic breakfast dates); and to Book People for being exactly the sort of independent bookstore that Willow and Evie would just *die* to visit.

Fourth, that there would be no new stories if there wasn't already so much wonderful work out there to draw upon for inspiration. This book was heavily influenced by the following: *You've Got Mail*, *The Legend of Sleepy Hollow*, *RuPaul's Drag Race*, *Beetlejuice*, *The Shining*, and Nancy Drew. Special thanks to Lance Mullins (and Carrie D'Cross) for helping me to bring Leo and Leonata to life.

Fifth, that I would be absolutely nothing without the love and support of the three people who matter most of all: Mark, Sophia, and Alex. I love you guys more than Halloween (which, as those who know me can attest, is a truly frightening amount!) Special thanks to (then-baby) Alex for refusing to sleep the night before his uncle's wedding, giving me no choice but to walk him around the Fairmont San Jose for hours in the dead of night—in that type of situation, it's impossible to *not* start brainstorming a book about a haunted hotel.

Finally, that I will never adequately be able to express my gratitude to the people who pick up my books and decide to spend some time with them—but I'll try anyway! Readers! Thank you for taking a chance on this story! I hope it haunts you (in the best possible way) for many years to come.

ABOUT THE AUTHOR

Cory Putman Oakes was born in Basel, Switzerland, but grew up in Northern California. In addition to *The Second-Best Haunted Hotel on Mercer Street*, she's also the author of two other middle grade novels (*Dinosaur Boy* and *Dinosaur Boy Saves Mars*) as well as two young adult novels (*Witchtown* and *The Veil*). Cory is a former lawyer and an aspiring teacher who holds degrees from UCLA and Cornell Law School. She lives in Austin, Texas, with her husband, Mark; their kids, Sophia and Alex; two cats; and a one-eyed hedgehog named Professor Pickles. If Cory were to come back as a ghost, she would find herself a beautiful, well-stocked library to haunt so she could spend her afterlife reading and snuggling some sort of ghost animal (like Cuddles).

ABOUT THE ILLUSTRATOR

Jane Pica is an illustrator who has been drawing since she was a little kid. She's a big fan of warm tea, Broadway soundtracks, and Disney movies, and she loves to draw characters that have big personalities. She lives and works as a freelance illustrator in Dubai.